RECONSTRUCTED
YANKEE

RECONSTRUCTED YANKEE

Frank Crowe —

*To a descendant of 48th
PA Vols. Hope you enjoy the
tale!*

JACK MAPLES

*Jack Maples
2001*

**CORINTHIAN
BOOKS**

Mt. Pleasant, S.C.

Publisher's Cataloguing-in-Publication
(Provided by Quality Books, Inc.):

Maples, Jack.
    Reconstructed Yankee / Jack Maples. — 1st ed.
    p. cm.
    ISBN 1-929175-29-9 (hc)
    ISBN 1-929175-48-5 (pb)

       1. United States—History—Civil War, 1861-1865—
African Americans—Fiction. 2. Freedmen—Southern
States—Fiction. 3. Confederate States of America—
Fiction. 4. African Americans—Southern States—
History—19th century—Fiction. 5. Historical fiction.
I Title.

PS3563.A65R43 2002   813'.6
                        QBI01-700794

Corinthian Books
an imprint of The Côté Literary Group
P.O. Box 1898
Mt. Pleasant, S.C. 29465-1898
(843) 881-6080
http://www.corinthianbooks.com

Contents

To the most forgotten soldiers of the Southern War for Independence for whom McIver's words are most oddly prophetic.

"We have shed our best blood. . . . We have made all this sacrifice and have been so wonderfully successful, some of our own people at home, for whom we have endured so much, are at last about to turn against us and aid our enemies, to do, what [the enemy] acknowledge they are unable to do, subjugate us."
Captain James D. McIver
26th North Carolina
August 13, 1863

THE BLACKSMITHS

Many people don't believe that there were any black Confederate soldiers. They say that would be impossible. Why would a Negro fight to keep slavery? And even more outlandish, why would a Negro who fought for the Union at the beginning of the war change sides? A black Confederate who claimed to be a reconstructed Yankee is too hard to believe.

Many of the war records have been destroyed or changed, but that doesn't change the truth of the matter. Muster rolls don't include teamsters and body servants, traditional roles for blacks. In some cases, "Private" has been crossed out and "teamster" or "body servant" written in. But I actually knew a reconstructed Yankee—a black soldier who changed sides. He was my grandfather.

His story began in a blacksmith shop in Haywood County, North Carolina, almost twenty-five years before the war. Two men worked the shop. One was white and the other black. The white man was in charge, but in every way, the two appeared equally expert in their craft. Each took a turn pumping the bellows and rolling the metal in the glowing coals before returning to the anvil to shape it into its desired form. They moved in an efficient rhythm born of experience.

Along the walls on one end of the shop were castings and finished metal parts. These included the barrel hoops and wagon wheels, as well as rifle barrels, pistol stocks, and horseshoes. Barrel staves and wheel spokes were stacked neatly on the floor or leaned into the corners. The men were more than blacksmiths and gunsmiths. They were also coopers and wheelwrights.

Each man showed the scars from over a decade of working at his trade. The pinkish brown scars on the arms and face of the black man showed more distinctly against his darker skin. Although not much lighter and equally leathered from the sun, the burn marks on the white man seemed to better blend with his skin.

The two had known each other since boyhood. Their fathers had worked this shop together until a few months before, when the typhus took them both. Now, these men in their late twenties carried on, struggling to do the work of four, since only the two of them remained.

John, the white man, stopped working, as the black man was about to return his work to the fire. "Jonah, I have a puzzlement."

"Yes, sir. I suspected you did by the way you been acting."

John was unsure about how to approach the dilemma. He and Jonah could usually talk about anything. "I reckon you can help me, but I gotta ask some questions. I'll ask you plain as I can and hope you'll answer me the same."

"I'll try."

"That Sissy girl you talk with at church—think you might like to jump the broom with her?"

Jonah didn't let on that the question startled him. "Might," he answered.

John knew he had to play it out just right. "Seems like she might like to marry you herself."

"Don't rightly know. Haven't asked her."

"Well, do you intend to ask?" John asked expectantly.

Jonah smiled, "Like you asked Miss Susan to marry you?"

"Exactly."

"Dunno how I can. That all there is to your puzzlement?"

As well as John knew Jonah, the man surely could frustrate the pajezzus out of him. "Well partly," John said intending to go on.

"I'm still listening, Massuh," Jonah interrupted. Jonah was John's slave now that his father had passed on, but John hated to be reminded of it. He and Jonah had played, fished, hunted, and caught hell together. That was a big part of his puzzlement.

John turned and thrust the metal piece he was working back into the fire and pumped hard on the bellows. Jonah's mother, Ruth, appeared at the door as he pulled down the second stroke. She was a small, almost frail looking, woman. John's mother had died giving birth to his sister. When John's sister died of typhus two weeks before his father, Jonah's mother was left to once again be the only woman to care for the household.

"Don't you boys bicker none," she said loudly enough to be heard over the noise of their hammering. "Breakfast is ready, so come on to the house now."

They knew better than to argue. John would have to finish later. Jonah favored his father and was taller and stronger than John, who took after his mother's side of the family. With Ruth leading the way, they acted like small children dragged away from their favorite game.

As some of the few craftsmen in the valley, the family, although not rich, fared well. Breakfast reflected their better-than-average financial condition. Hardboiled eggs, ham, corn mush, fried apples, fresh milk, and bread made up that morning's fare. Of course, there was plenty of hot tea.

John picked up the questioning as they returned to the shop. "You can't marry Sissy proper 'cause you're both slaves. So, jumping the broom is all you got."

"I know my place, John," was Jonah's indignant reply. "And besides, I dunno how we can even be proper without yore help. Sissy's massuh never'd let 'er over here by her own self."

"That's my puzzlement. Since yore an inherited slave, it's illegal for me to sell you. Even if I could, I'd be a fool." John thrust the hot metal piece he was working on into the water. The water sizzled, and steam came up to momentarily hide John from Jonah's view.

"No reason you can't buy Sissy, if you would," Jonah offered. "Mama needs the help. Course, you going to marry Miss Susan."

"Jonah, that's exactly what I did."

"Did what?"

John looked Jonah straight in the eyes. "Bought Sissy. And I'm gonna make her my indenture not my slave. Yore gonna help her pay it off. That includes the manumission bond. It'll take you some time."

Jonah beamed.

John's second surprise would wait until their wedding day, two months later. The wedding gift would be Jonah's freedom as well as Sissy's. It was a costly gift. The manumission bond was $1,000 against Jonah's "good behavior."

At the wedding, John also renewed the promise of Sissy's freedom once the cost of her indenture and bond were repaid. John and Susan Parker then helped Jonah and Sissy Parker build their house. Jonah and Sissy's house would be identical to John and Susan's.

John was not an abolitionist. His neighbors now would look at him that way, but John saw Jonah's freedom differently. It went beyond their having grown up together. It was a practical matter. Free colored folks had a hard time. Most whites wouldn't or couldn't pay them a living wage. A free Negro took too many risks to leave his own community in search of work.

Many whites were "alarmists." Nat Turner's rebellion made them see slaves and free Negroes alike as a threat. John wanted to have Jonah see him as a partner. It was good for business. He knew Jonah would work better for a fair wage than as a slave dependent on John's good graces.

The increased business proved John right. He hired on extra help in the spring and summer. Jonah ran the woodworking operations in spite of initial objections of the white workers, who resented taking orders from a black man. Several men came and went before two were found who appreciated Jonah's skill.

Eighteen months after marrying Jonah, Sissy gave birth to a son, Caleb. Seven months later Jonah paid the last of Sissy's indenture. Two months after Caleb's birth, John and Susan's son, Thomas, was born. Like their fathers, Tom and Caleb played, fished, hunted, and caught hell together. In the next five years, Susan had three more daughters. The youngest, Mary, died young. Sissy bore two daughters and another son. Lizbeth, her second daughter, died of the fever when she was six.

Susan, the daughter of a schoolmaster, taught the children and Sissy to read and cipher. Most of the schooling came at night after the day's work was done or when bad weather kept them inside. The education went on year 'round.

By the time they were ten, Tom and Caleb started to work in the shop. At first, it was simple chores with Caleb's seven-year-old brother, George, shadowing their every step. Then, ever so slowly, they learned the trades in which their fathers were expert. Both boys showed talent as gunsmiths.

By the time they were seventeen, Tom and Caleb were making guns for the locals and building a genuine reputation. In only two years, wealthy men from all over the Carolinas, northeast Georgia, and eastern Tennessee sought them out to make customized weapons.

The boys were more than good. They made guns that rivaled the best in their part of the country. They could improve on any design that came their way.

Then, when they were almost twenty, the states of the Deep South began seceding from the Union. After rejecting a state convention for secession in February, North Carolina was admitted into the Confederacy in May 1861. In Virginia, the first battle at Manassas followed in July. With so many men and boys from the highlands enlisting, Tom and Caleb didn't worry about going off to fight at first.

Conscription began in April 1862. Being a smith was a crucial skill for the area's economy. At first, Tom was exempt when Haywood County authorities came around to complete local "enrollments." The exemption did not help his reputation as a white man who, like his father, was seen as a friend of a nigrah.

Pro-secession politicians like Thomas Clingman used fear of a free African population to build opposition to abolitionism. The notion stuck in the minds of most folks in the South. Since John had voluntarily and privately freed Jonah, people suspected him of being a pro-Unionist, Abolitionist, and most likely, a Black Republican as well. He did all he could to prove otherwise; nonetheless, the suspicion prevailed.

Living in the North Carolina highlands didn't mean that the Parkers escaped the consequences of the war. Bushwhackers and loyalist guerrillas roamed the highlands or swept into the valleys, terrorizing those who disagreed with their position. Union and Confederate deserters wandered through the counties seeking shelter in the rugged mountains. Isolated as they often were, family homesteads were at their mercy. The two families of Parkers lived neither in town nor in isolation. They were in between and close to all.

Those whose sympathies favored the Confederacy were panicked by the Federal capture of the Cumberland Gap. An invasion from Kentucky through East Tennessee would bring the Yankees straight into western North Carolina. Reprisals against those suspected of Yankee sympathies followed. The Parkers avoided the wrath of the pro-secessionists.

The reprisals were only an extension of the threats that existed before the war. A drunken sheriff who supported the Democrats had shot an equally drunk former Whig, because alcohol had brought their true emotions to the surface. In Yancey County, a pro-Union Baptist minister turned over his congregation to another before being ridden out of town on a rail, but he came to no physical harm. It was only intimidation.

As word arrived of the Confederate victory at Manassas, tensions eased. Then, as the winter of 1862 progressed, the losses at Forts Henry and Donelson, Shiloh, and Island No. 10, brought them back again. Murders and senseless destruction all over western North Carolina were reported daily into the spring and throughout the summer of 1862. Unlike the arguments before the war when the opponents faced each other openly, the terrorism came from faceless banshees shrieking from out of the darkness. The young Parker men had to take a stand and for Tom, it came early in 1862.

"Pa," Tom said almost like a question.

"Yes, son."

"Talked some with Alexander Jones when I delivered those wheels to Hendersonville yesterday. I reckon it's time I head north."

"What makes you think that?"

"Jones says since there're so few of them, the mouths of Union men are almost completely gagged. A year ago, two men in three voted against secession. Now, these men have vanished. That, or else, they're supporting secession."

John thought he knew where Tom was headed. "Are you a Union man?"

"Pa, I'm on the fence like you are, but I keep my sympathies among my true friends. Good Lord knows we neither one favor slavery. Not with Jonah and Caleb being like near family. Matter a fact, I don't like those wealthy planters bringing their slaves up here in the summertime."

"I feel the same way, Tom, and you know it. But the Lincolnites stand for some things I can't abide."

Tom hesitated a moment. "I'm no Unionist or Lincolnite either. What I do believe is that secession and slavery ain't right. These Confederates believe in both. Given my druthers, I'd just as soon be left alone."

"We agree on a lot of things," John said, "but I still don't know why you gotta go north."

"'Cause Jones told me they're coming to enroll me day after tomorrow. They're also gonna be looking to see if I'll try to run," Tom said, watching the color drain from his father's face. "If I've gotta fight, it'll be for the Yankees. Pa, I need to know what you think."

John leaned against the windowsill. "They're enrolling you 'cause Jonah and me are too old, and they won't enroll Caleb. We don't have a reason to keep you exempt."

"I can't fight with the Rebels, Pa." Tom struggled to keep his voice steady. "I gotta figger how to get to Kentucky where there's Union troops. Caleb wants to come with me."

"The Rebs have cavalry and militia on all the main roads and at all the passes." John objected. "You know the stories about Unionists being slaughtered when they try to get North." He sighed. "We'll talk after supper, after Jonah and Caleb get back from Waynesville." John's tone indicated that he was not about to discuss the matter any further.

Jonah and Caleb arrived just before sundown. It was evident from their somber faces that they, too, had discussed the situation. Sissy fixed supper—fresh baked bread, greens cooked with fatback, and a sweet potato pie with baked meringue. Susan brought a smoked ham.

Afterward, the men pushed back their chairs and sat in silence for a while. Then Jonah began. He didn't want Caleb to go. At the same time, he couldn't watch Tom go by himself. If Tom had to go, Caleb had to go with him. Tears filled Sissy's eyes, but she nodded in agreement. That much was settled quickly.

But should the boys try to make it North or should they join the Confederacy here and then "disappear"? If Tom and Caleb went North, they might never be able to return home. Fighting for the South conflicted with their beliefs. Going North seemed the only choice. The question was how? Several routes were discussed and quickly rejected. After an hour, they had not made much progress.

The decision was abruptly taken out of their hands. Boots clumped on the front porch followed by a soft knock. "Alexander sent me," said a voice. John got up to open the door.

"I'm Captain Bryson, 1st Tennessee National Guard. My horse and men will be riding up shortly. We've found that a real noisy unexpected visit tends to make the rabbit scoot."

Bryson was a known Union man. Local Confederates hated him. Knowing that Alexander Jones was a Unionist, John didn't seem surprised that Bryson had shown up. "Goldman Bryson of Cherokee County?" he asked.

"One and the same. I understand you got a boy here whose loyalties need protection from Rebel conscription."

"I'd heard you were in Knoxville. You have certainly arrived with timely haste." John said, and then offered, "Actually, we have two such men."

"Jones said Caleb probably would leave, too. We don't have much time. The locals will be watching the roads."

Tom and Caleb jumped up to pack their horses and gather

weapons and ammunition. Minutes later, Tom returned to the house. "Caleb'll be here shortly," he said as he stuffed clothes into a cloth bag.

Caleb arrived, followed by one of Bryson's men, who called out, "Cap'n, the Rebs are coming. Need to ride outta here." The boys quickly kissed their mothers and sisters goodbye. Their fathers hugged their sons in farewell.

Outside, the boys pulled themselves into the saddle and rode out at a gallop, riding as hard as their horses would go. They headed not west or north, but due east.

The next night, the Confederates caught up with them near Swannanoa Gap. Hearing them approach, Bryson's small column turned to face their pursuers. The force was reduced by the need for horse holders. The men hid behind trees and on the back side of a small slope.

Bryson kept Tom and Caleb with him. "Pick your shots boys. Least wise, best you can."

They were just off the road. Most of Bryson's men were off to the right. The fight would be with small arms and shotguns. Tom suspected that Bryson kept them near him because of their carbines.

The Confederate column—twice the size of Bryson's—came straight up the road. Unionist muzzles flashed. The Confederates wheeled about to fire in the direction of their attackers.

Tom and Caleb could barely tell where to aim. They fired rapidly at the flashes, but there was no way of telling if they hit anyone. Then came shotgun explosions. Bright bursts of light were followed by howls and screams. Tom saw the outline of an enemy rider. He squeezed the trigger and watched the man roll out of the saddle.

Caleb used the brief illumination to advantage. His shot struck the stock of a Confederate's shotgun. The man's gun fired into the air, lighting up the trail in a five-foot radius. Caleb recocked the carbine and fired again. The Confederate slumped over the horse's neck.

Until that moment, Caleb hadn't noticed the strong odor of black powder. It now filled his nostrils and burned his eyes.

He heard Bryson's "Good work, boys." Then another volley of pistol and shotgun fire burst from Bryson's men. The Confederate cavalry turned and retreated down the road. In the darkness, Bryson's men slipped away. Two men had been slightly wounded; no men had been seriously injured.

The following morning, militia from four counties continued the search for the Yankee column. As was their custom, Bryson's force had already returned to their homes. They formed up only when the need arose. Tom and Caleb began their journey north escorted only by Bryson himself.

Two weeks later in their home territory, another pro-Union man, who apparently didn't have the sense to keep his sympathies to himself, was scheduled to be hanged. The Federals sent a squad in from Tennessee to rescue him. Riding straight into Waynesville, they plucked the man out of harm's way. The message was clear: western North Carolina was vulnerable to Federal attack.

2

YANKEE PARTISANS

All that Bryson promised the boys was safe passage to an independent Union unit in east Tennessee, and even that wasn't guaranteed. If they were intercepted by Confederate patrols, Tom and Caleb were to say that they were catching up with General Hoke and the 21st North Carolina.

"Better to ride with the Rebs than to be hanged as traitors," Bryson said. "You always can slip away later. Lots of Confederate deserters are in the ranks of the Union army."

In Tennessee, Tom and Caleb could join a militia unit or go on to a Federal recruiting station. They already had decided to join the militia. A formal enlistment in the Union army was too great a break with their North Carolina kinsmen.

Bryson rode with them east of Buncombe County, taking them on lesser-known paths, and leaving them outside Marion. In the company of another of Bryson's men, they rode toward northwest Burnsville. Because of the Confederate patrols, they rode away from Paint Rock and avoided the main turnpike along the French Broad River.

At first they spent more time hiding than riding. Their route, taken in short segments, forced them up into rugged country.

They proceeded to Greenville, then crossed over the East Tennessee and Virginia Railroad. They entered Tennessee near the border of Madison and Yancey counties in North Carolina. It had been eight days since they left home.

Once in Tennessee, they continued northwest to Tazewell, then east to Jamestown. There they waited near a small farm for the militia to return. After a three-day wait, a message arrived that they were to return to the militia camp south of Tazewell.

Riding into the camp, they passed by several hundred dirty men in well-worn, if not raggedy, clothes. Most carried sidearms, shotguns, and a variety of knives. Their equipment was much like that carried by Bryson and his men. Very few appeared to have decent rifles or carbines. It was clearly an ill-equipped force and failed to impress Tom or Caleb. They dismounted at the tent of a rough-looking man chomping on a cigar.

"This here's Captain Beatty," a soldier said.

"They call me Tinker Dave," Beatty said. "Where y'all from?"

"North Carolina," Tom replied.

Ignoring simple courtesy, Beatty directed a second question at Tom, "Looking to jine up?"

"My name's Tom Parker. This man here's my friend, Caleb Parker."

"Don't take no niggers in this unit, lessen he's yore slave," Beatty answered.

Tom glanced at Caleb, and then looked back toward Beatty. "Caleb was born free. He ain't no slave. Guess we gotta look elsewhere, Caleb."

Looking at the carbines on the saddles, Beatty asked, "Kin he shoot?"

Caleb didn't say a word. He stepped back toward his horse and withdrew the carbine from its saddle holster. Picking up a handful of walnuts on a plate near where Beatty sat, Caleb walked to the fence. He placed the walnuts on the top rail, saving one for the fencepost. Turning around, Caleb carefully walked off thirty paces.

A few of Beatty's men laughed. One of them called out, "Them's not *black* walnuts!"

Another said, "Never seen a nigger could shoot!"

Caleb didn't flinch. He drew the carbine up to his shoulder, cocked the hammer, and squeezed the trigger slowly. The first shot exploded the walnut. The other two walnuts rocked slightly. Caleb pumped the lever to reload each time. The next two shots came quickly and with equal accuracy. Beatty's men were quiet now, but one drunk yelled, "Hey, black boy, there's still one left."

The gun was lowered as Caleb turned and grinned. Bringing the gun to his shoulder one more time, he fired and the walnut sprang up in the air. As it reached the crest of its rise, Caleb fired again. The walnut exploded in mid-air. "Tom shoots almost as good as me," Caleb said as he scooped up the reusable casings near his feet. He turned and started walking back to his horse.

"Man simply don't appreciate talent," Tom said loudly. "Guess we'll find us another unit."

"And you've already found it, gentlemen," another voice replied.

Tom and Caleb both turned in the direction of the voice. "I'm the Reverend William B. Carter," the man said stepping out from behind a small group of soldiers.

Carter was well known. He had come across the North Carolina border to preach at their pro-Union Methodist Church in Waynesville before the war. Because Jonah and Sissy had to sit in the back, all the Parkers sat there. Noticing them, the Reverend Carter commented on the way the two families stuck together.

Carter was known for being more than a Unionist. The previous fall, Carter had led a raid that destroyed five of nine bridges on the East Tennessee and Virginia Railroad. The raid was to be in support of an attack that was planned by the Union general, William T. Sherman. On November 8, the Union attack stalled, and Sherman rescinded his orders to General George Thomas. Carter went forward anyway and became an instant hero among East Tennessee Unionists.

"Well I'll be," Carter said. "I remember you boys from Waynesville." Tom and Caleb look at each other in disbelief at being recognized.

"I'm Tom Parker, and this here's Caleb Parker."

Carter smiled. "Y'all must be those gunmaking Parker boys I keep hearing about."

Caleb interjected, "We begun making guns 'bout the time you came to church."

"That was only about five years ago," Carter said with surprise. "You boys learn fast." They ducked their heads in acknowledgment.

"My men mostly use paper cartridges," Carter continued. "Do you have enough ammunition for your weapons?"

This time it was Tom who answered, "Yes, sir. As long as there's powder and lead, we can make our own. We have plenty of empty casings and the tools we need."

"What kind of carbine is that?" Carter asked.

"We built them ourselves," Tom said. "Got the idea after seeing one like them when we went to Charleston in the fall of '59."

Carter was curious. "Looks a little like a Spencer, but it's different somehow."

"Lots different, but that's what the man in Charleston called it," Caleb said.

"Anyways," Tom continued, "he gave us each a bullet after showing how it worked. Fired it at a cotton bale. We didn't tell them we made guns, just acted like boys at a circus."

Caleb picked up the story. "So when we got back home, we took a bullet apart to sees how it works. We'd seen lotsa paper and linen cartridges. Metal ones, too. Took a few weeks 'til we got it figgered. We couldn't make the rim fire bullets. Center fires we can make, so we planned the gun around that kind of ammunition."

"Sure, but y'all still didn't have the gun," Carter said.

"The gun was the easy part. The Spencer loaded with a long tube in the stock. Too hard. The lever, ejector, and breechblock we understood already. What needed fixing was the loading part," Tom said.

Carter nodded for him to continue. Caleb again removed the carbine from the saddle holster. "See this here on the side," Tom said as he pressed down on a grooved plate on the stock near the hammer to reveal an inner chamber. "We built the tube and the spring inside. The bullets go in here backwards. First one in is the last one fired."

"Seems light," Carter said as he held it in one hand.

"That's another difference. Ours is shorter. Only 42 inches and it fires the .44 pin fires not .52 rim fires. With the shorter barrel, Tom and me used three smaller bands to hold the barrel."

Tom interrupted. "Weighs 'bout eight and a half pounds loaded with ten rounds. Spencer weighs at least ten pounds and only has seven rounds."

Carter smiled. "How many of these did you make?"

"Just four," Caleb answered. "Took nigh unto six months on and off to get the molds right. Then we had to fit 'em together special."

"Caleb and me each got one and so did our fathers.

"So why do you save the casings?" Carter asked.

Tom exclaimed, "You sure have lotsa questions! Pa and Jonah can make more, but the stuff's too heavy for us to carry. We have primed blanks, more primes, molds, crimps, and such. With them, powder, and lead, we can assemble more ammunition using the press we can carry in our saddlebags. Just need to put the press back together again. Wasting the casings is something we can't afford to do."

"You can buy .44s, but indulge my curiosity just once more," the Reverend asked. "How long to make another?"

"Don't trust store-bought ammunition. As for the guns, now we have the molds, 'bout a week. It's slow work. Our pistols use the same bullets, but they're revolvers."

Carter laughed. "And what do you call these guns?"

Tom and Caleb looked at each other grinning. "Parkers. What else?"

Carter shook his head, then he turned to the others and called out, "Mount up, boys! We're leaving!" Turning back to Tom and Caleb, he said, "I'd be pleased if you'd ride with us. Them carbines of yours might come in right handy."

About forty-five men, including Tom and Caleb, were in the militia that left camp with Carter. No flags flew at the head of the column. Carter explained that they didn't want to be identified at a distance. Surprise was a critical element in their operations.

Riding three abreast, Carter kept Tom and Caleb at the head of the column with Tom in the middle and Caleb on the left. The horses proceeded at a slow walk. The boys were grateful for the easier pace in daylight after a week in the saddle riding mostly at night.

Carter led the column down the main road for less than five miles before turning off onto a trail sheltered by the trees, keeping them out of sight. They went into a column of twos.

Tom stayed with Carter and Caleb paired off with an older man.

"We usually ride alone in small groups," Carter began. "If you'd of come by later, we'd been gone. That was the first time we'd rode with Tinker Dave. I'd druther it was the last."

Tom asked the obvious question. "Why's that, Cap'n?"

"I see myself as a partisan. You know I don't like slavery. For me, this war's about ending it altogether. Cain't say the same for Tinker Dave. Claims he's pro-Union. Gentler folks'd call him a guerrilla. For myself, I think he's a murderer."

Caleb's question came from behind. "Then why'd y'all ride with him?"

Carter half-turned in his saddle. "This time we didn't have a choice. His militia was the only one available, and we needed extra men. Usually, Tinker holes up in the mountains on the East Fork of the Obey River. It's a tough place to get too. He don't like coming this far east."

Carter paused a moment. "I'd rather ride with David Fry, but he got sloppy and got himself captured in March. We got the Lick Creek Bridge together back in '61. He's a good soldier. Both of us went to the Unionist Convention meetings in Knoxville and Greenville earlier that year. My first choice is scouting for my brother. That's Sam, not J.P. He's a general now."

"Guess it's our turn for asking questions," Tom said. "Just what is it we're doing, Cap'n?"

Carter nodded. "Fair enough!" He added with a smile, "Most men call me Reverend or Bill. Don't take much to being called Captain." The boys already knew that the Carters were wealthy and came from their namesake Carter County, Tennessee. Carter didn't mention those simple facts, but described the founding of his unit.

The previous July, Bill's brother, J. P. Carter, went to Kentucky to meet with Lieutenant William Nelson, who began recruiting men from Tennessee and Kentucky in June 1861. J.P.

wanted weapons to arm Union loyalists in East Tennessee. With the Confederates blocking all the major routes into that area, Nelson didn't want to risk the seizure of supplies in a failed smuggling attempt. Nelson told J.P. to bring the men to Camp Dick Robinson, in Kentucky, for training.

Sam Carter joined Nelson and J.P. after being recalled from his position as a lieutenant in the Federal navy. Lincoln initially had commissioned him in the army as a colonel with orders to evacuate Union loyalists out of East Tennessee.

Sherman had taken command of the Army of the Cumberland in August. He appointed Union General George H. Thomas to direct training operations at Camp Dick Robinson in September. Meanwhile, Bill Carter remained in Tennessee to observe the Confederate treatment of loyalists. He also organized loyalists and aided their escape to Kentucky until he was forced to flee himself.

Carter wrote a report on loyalist suffering in East Tennessee. His report included the plan to burn or destroy the nine East Tennessee and Virginia Railroad bridges. He then went to Washington to discuss his plan with President Lincoln, Secretary of War Simon Cameron, and General McClellan. He had hoped that a successful raid would cut off East Tennessee from the rest of the state. Further, he hoped to deny the Confederacy a means of communication and transportation between the west, northern Georgia, and, most importantly, Richmond.

With the approval of Washington, and agreement by Sherman and Thomas, Carter went back into East Tennessee. Captains David Fry and William Cross, of Greene and Scott County respectively, went with him. When Sherman rescinded Thomas' orders, the East Tennesseans were left to their own devices.

Union loyalists in the area considered the raid a success, but in the absence of the planned invasion, nothing more came of it. Carter believed the entire episode to be bungled after he left. He also felt that the four bridges that weren't destroyed compounded the failure. Neither Tom nor Caleb was aware of the attempts on those other four bridges.

Only two men were sent to Bridgeport, Alabama, to wreck the Memphis and Charleston Bridge over the Tennessee River. The bridge was heavily guarded, and the two men could not get close enough to achieve their objective. Events at the Watauga River Bridge in Carter County and the Tennessee River Bridge near Loudon paralleled those in Bridgeport.

Carter was bitter about what happened at the Holston River Bridge outside Strawberry Plains. It was nothing less than inadequate planning and atrocious fortune. A single guard surprised the thirteen men who were on the bridge and wounded two. The remaining eleven men, out of matches, decided they couldn't blow up or burn the bridge. They fled.

"Stupidity and cowardice!" Carter exclaimed. "Don't know which is worse. Eleven men skedaddled because of a single Rebel guard. Anyways, ever since, that's what we do. Not the bungled raids, but the scouting, raiding, and screening for the Army."

"What're we doing now?" Tom asked.

"We're gonna find out. Tomorrow or the next day, I expect to run into General Thomas," Carter replied. "I got another question for you, though. Bryson had men bring you all the way to Tazewell. He doesn't do that cuz he wants his men staying close to home. Usually, they only come to a meeting spot south of Greenville. Y'all being taken to Tinker Dave's another puzzle. You know why?"

"Cain't rightly say," Tom answered.

"Me, neither," added Caleb.

Carter said, "Then, that's three of us not knowing."

Tom seemed to be brooding. "Why'd you call Tinker Dave a murderer?"

"He's from Fentress County. West of there's Rebel country, in spite of the Union occupation. Just south is White County. A bushwhacker named Champ Ferguson's there. Champ and Tinker're cut from the same cloth. So's William Clift, another one claiming to be a Union man. He's got a big farm in Hamilton County outside Chattanooga," Carter said choosing his words carefully. "For them, this war's an excuse."

"Not sure I know exactly what you mean, Reverend," Tom said.

Carter let out a weary sigh. "There're men like Beatty, Clift, and Ferguson on both sides. They're filled with hate. Out on this last raid, we were destroying supplies and tearing down telegraph lines. Tangled with some Rebel cavalry and militia, too. That's just fighting a war."

He raised his hand to halt the column. There was a clearing visible ahead. The main trail bore right and another trail came in from the left. Both appeared to circle the large open field in front.

Tom didn't speak. His instincts as a hunter told him that now was a time to be silent. Carter eased his horse forward cautiously. He surveyed the land making a decision to cross in the open or to take one of the trails. Not satisfied with what he could see, Carter removed a small glass from his inner coat pocket. Peering through the glass, and adjusting the focus twice, he turned back to take the new trail.

"We'll go west, just to be safe. I don't like being exposed." Carter led the column silently for about twenty minutes before he spoke again. "I wasn't sure if there were horses on the other side or not. Lemme finish answering your question."

Tom said, "Thank you, Reverend."

Carter smiled. He liked this earnest young man. "While we're out, Beatty came across a family he knew. A secesh family with the men folk not home. He burned the house and other buildings to the ground. As he left, he shot both their slaves in the leg. There weren't no call to do it. I don't make war on families, he does."

"Secesh are doing the same thing to loyalists," Tom said. "Heard 'bout it plenty."

"Don't make it right, son. 'Sides, the reason he burned the place, and Tinker told me this himself, was because he and this man had been feuding for years. Back in January '62, a Reb named Bledsoe came through Beatty's farm. They looted the place and threatened his wife. He didn't take kindly to it."

"So this man'll come back and burn Beatty's place if he can," Caleb interjected.

"I reckon so," Carter answered. "Champ's killing secesh and loyalists alike based on his personal grudges. It's a matter of revenge. His men do the same. That ain't war, that's killing. Tinker's caught up in it. I don't make war on families. My men only attack their armies and militia. Can't say that Sherman shares my beliefs."

3

FIRST ENGAGEMENT

In the two days and nights that followed, Tom and Caleb got to know the other men riding with Bill Carter. One, named Levi, was barely eighteen, and two others were only seventeen. Most of the rest were grown men with children, but a few were mountain hermits, coarse and rough of manner. Very few could read and write. Their interests were plain and simple. The war for them was a matter of patriotism and loyalty, as it had been for their grandfathers in the American Revolution. Given their age and experience, these older men saw Tom and Caleb as mere untested boys.

Riding into Camp Dick Robinson, Tom and Caleb understood how large the war really was. They had seen it only through the eyes of a small community. The camp was alive with thousands of men, escaped slaves, and camp followers. Forges and wagon-making shops were everywhere, and any one of them was bigger than the two men had ever seen. There were endless numbers of corrals filled with horses and mules. All they could do was gawk.

Then, too, there were tents offering liquor, gambling, and other pleasures. Tinker Dave's small camp was a pale comparison. Carter stopped the column in front of a quartermaster's tent and went in. The men remained mounted. After a few moments, Carter emerged and remounted his horse. Motioning the column forward, Carter led his men to the eastern edge of the camp. There they found a row of two-man tents. A larger officer's tent was in the middle of one row.

Tom and Caleb were given a tent at the end of the row, fifteen yards from the tether line for the horses. Before they could finish unsaddling their mounts, several former slaves appeared, offering to groom the horses for a modest fee. Their offers were readily accepted. The carbines and the saddlebags with the ammunition-making supplies went with Tom and Caleb to their tent.

The mess that night was good. Whatever it was, the sweet-smelling meat in the stew made the meal. One of the men had the makings for cornbread. Grease scooped from the stew helped season the iron skillet. Caleb said that the cornbread rivaled his mother's.

That night the men relaxed—singing, dancing, and joking. Hushed tones were no longer necessary. Caleb remembered it as a night of enjoymen. In the days and nights of the year that followed, other, more terrible, memories would torture him for a lifetime.

After a while, most of the men drifted away to their tents. Tom and Caleb still sat by the fire resting against a large log.

A man named John Cobb sat down next to them. "Heard you talking with the Reverend 'bout Tinker Dave and Champ Ferguson."

"You couldn't help but hear," Caleb replied, "being you was riding back of me."

Cobb sat up, leaned over, and pushed a twig into the fire. He used the flaming twig to light a mangled cigar that he pulled from his vest pocket. "Tinker's not the only bad one. I just escaped from Morgan, so I kin tell you about what I seen Ferguson and Philpot do."

"Who's Philpot?" Tom asked.

"Rains Philpot, one of Ferguson's lieutenants. Sometimes he rides with his own militia. Me and two others got caught by Morgan just seven weeks ago. Ferguson caught four other Union men. One of 'em was a man named Henry Sells, who was a good friend of Tinker's."

Caleb said, "Was? He and Tinker gotta grudge?"

"No, I said 'was' cuz Sells is dead. Philpot and Ferguson took all their prisoners outta the camp one night. Sells came back last with Philpot leading the horse with his body slung across it. Next morning they asked if we wanted to go down that road or jine the Confederacy."

"Take it you jined the Rebs," Tom interrupted.

Cobb smiled, "That I did, but I got let go the next morning. Kept Tinker's brother though. Shot him in the arms and legs, then hung him. Tinker's got more of a grudge now."

"So what are you saying?" Tom asked.

The voice that came from behind startled all of them. "That there's ugliness and brutality on both sides," Carter said without expression. Because this was a militia unit and not regular army, no one had to stand up or salute when an officer joined them.

"An' that's the truth, Reverend," Cobb replied.

"Cobb, I agree. We've all heard the stories and lost friends and kinfolks. If we take it personal, we'll be fighting long after this war's over."

"And the way things are going, we *will* be."

"If you don't mind, Cobb, I need to talk with these boys alone. No secrets, we've had the same talk."

Cobb stood up and offered a casual salute. Carter waved him off, "No need for that, son."

Cobb strolled off. Carter turned back to Tom and Caleb, "Let's walk over there. We won't be interrupted."

"Sure enough, Reverend," Tom said. "What's this about?"

Carter didn't answer. He just kept walking away from the camp and into the field. They were halfway between the camp and the sentries at the outer lines, when Carter turned right and walked another five yards. In the moonlight, the boys could see logs laid out in neat rows. Carter sat on one. Tom and Caleb chose another facing Carter.

"Y'all never fought with me before," Carter said.

Tom said, "We ain't never fought with no one."

"I know that and I'm not gonna give you no preaching about being brave. That's up to y'all. We need to talk about how I fight and the signals you need to watch out for."

"How do you fight?" Caleb asked.

"Most of the time we ambush. We lay in wait and strike fast. The horses are left behind. One man keeps four horses. I leave the younger ones to do it. Ordinarily, that would be your job. Fact is, I need you and your carbines."

Caleb stiffened. Tom leaned back while placing his hands on the log beside him. Neither spoke and waited for Carter to continue. "Good enough. When I touch my cap, everyone fires at once. Two men—and I'm usually one of them—target their leaders. Try not to make it look obvious. Only a few men know the orders."

"You're sharing with us 'cause you want us to do it?" Tom asked.

Carter stared straight at both of the young men. "Yes."

"I'll do it," Caleb said.

Tom added, "So'll I."

"Don't try and kill 'em. Just keep them from leading men again any time soon," Carter added. "I don't want the others to know 'cause if they know, the Rebs'll do the same."

"I understand," Tom said and Caleb nodded. "Can you tell us where we're going, Reverend?"

"Behind Reb lines is all I can say. We'll ride out late tomorrow." Carter stood up. "There's more I need to tell you. This ain't the army. My rules are easier. You serve 'cause you want to not 'cause you have to."

Caleb asked, "You mean we can leave whenever we want to?"

"Just tell me when you want to go. I may ask you to wait or may tell you to go ahead. If I need you to stay, it'll be for a reason. You can stay out of any fight that might include friends or kin on the other side."

Tom, standing up, said, "I won't shoot anyone who ain't armed."

"Neither will I, but sometimes odd things happen," said Carter. "If I catch a known murderer, I won't show any mercy. We don't have time to wait for the court. Morgan, Ferguson, and Philpot are three examples that come to mind."

Tom and Caleb shook their heads, and Carter continued, "I understand your discomfort. You don't know the people those men killed for no reason at all. I knew George Woods, Bill Allen, Andy Robbins, and Henry Sells. I knew Tinker's brother, too. Killing unarmed prisoners is murder. I ever find Philpot or Ferguson, I show them the same lack of respect."

"Ain't we better than them that way?" Tom asked.

"That Reb general Zollicoffer thinks we're ignorant and backward. Problem is Sherman, Thomas, and most Yankee officers don't think us much better," Carter said bitterly. "They don't much care if we're secesh or loyal. Us mountain people just don't matter, 'less we're needed or cause trouble for their side."

Caleb said, "Kind of like the way slaves is treated. Long as they're invisible or doing their work, nobody cares much."

"True enough, except the slaves and free Negroes are seen as less than the mountain folk. Inside the army, our people get the worst work and more punishment. Being with me, at least you'll be treated fair," Carter answered. He walked off.

Tom sat down again. "What you think, Caleb?"

"You've any idea what this fight's 'bout," Caleb asked.

Tom shook his head, "Can make lots of guesses, but cain't rightly figger."

Caleb responded, "Me, neither. None of the guesses make full sense."

Silhouetted by a half moon and the campfires of Camp Dick Robinson, they sat silent for several minutes. The noise of the camp was soft in the distance. They could see groups of men breaking up and going to their tents. The silence was broken by one gunshot followed by two more.

"Some of the boys are getting' rowdy," Tom said dryly.

Tom could see Caleb's smile. "Best we're here, then."

"Damn right. Reckon, we could find us a mess of trouble over there."

"Ain't no reckoning 'bout it. We already found a mess of trouble. Don't need to add to it none."

"You skeered?"

"Sure am," said Caleb. "Pa said I'd be. Warned me 'bout folks like Tinker Dave, too. I know my place as a nigrah. Your family always treated us right. In town and 'round other white folks though, I'm careful. Thought sure one of Dave's men was gonna shoot me for being uppity. Never counted on gettin' respect."

Tom hesitated. "Carter got us outta there before things got bad. You didn't just own a better gun. You made it your own self. They saw you shoot better than them with their own eyes, too. They'd a rather killed you than admit it. I don't trust all of the Reverend's men neither. Watch your back."

Tom knew he didn't have to say that, but he needed to. The warning surprised Caleb. They both knew that a so-called free person of color was neither as free as a white nor as beholding as a slave. Rather, they were suspect by both.

Jonah had told his son what slavery was like. John had treated Jonah as a friend and almost as a brother. Still, there was a difference between feeling almost free and actually being free. The two men acted like master and slave even after Jonah was freed. Tom and Caleb, however, had been raised like brothers, and the respect for each other was deep.

Caleb knew he could never own another person, given the chance. He'd heard stories from the slaves in town during the summer, when they came with their masters from the Piedmont and the coast. Some bragged about how well they got on while others told of mistreatment, beatings, and rape.

The worst stories were told about the black masters. Free persons of color, who saw their fortune in owning, illegally breeding, and selling slaves, were hated above all others. These were not the blacks who bought friends and kin to set them free. These added to the misery of their people and treated them worse than the whites did.

Caleb had read some of the speeches of Frederick Douglass. So had Tom. They had talked about them and argued a little, too. At church, they heard more about what Douglass believed. Most speakers were unkind in their appraisal. For Caleb, most of what Douglass said made sense. Knowing how uneducated the slaves were, Caleb couldn't figure how they'd make do without the protection of their masters. Still, he couldn't make right the practice of one man owning another.

For Caleb, this war still had to be fought for setting his people free and allowing them to become real Americans. That much of Douglass he agreed with. What he'd seen of the Union men so far told him they didn't share his belief. Tom had said it best, Caleb thought. He just wanted North Carolina to be left alone. Grudges had nothing to do with this war. The well-to-do on both sides wanted to protect their wealth. The poor had to find their own reasons to believe in this war. For many, it was a chance to settle some scores and maybe get the better of it in the bargain. No matter who won, Caleb couldn't see what it would gain for him. Seemed like he had more to lose than to gain.

"What're we gonna do?" Tom asked, interrupting Caleb's thoughts.

"'Less you planning on going home to hide in the mountains, I reckon we're gonna do some fighting real soon," Caleb replied.

"I don't know if I want to shoot Rebs any more than I wanted to shoot Yankees."

"What 'bout fighting for the Union itself?" Caleb asked.

"What Union?" Tom said coldly. "We live in the mountains, a long way from Washington and Boston or Richmond. I'm beginning to think I'm a Carolinian before I'm an American. Home counts for a lot."

"So, what're we gonna do?"

"Dunno, Caleb. I just dunno." Tom's words sounded weary, discouraged. "You're right about going home. We'd have to join the deserters and escaped prisoners in the mountains. That's not much of a life neither."

"I'd rather fight than hide out like that."

"We don't have much choice." Tom stood up and walked toward their tent. Caleb followed silently.

They awoke at sunrise as the camp began to stir. Tom found a bucket of water so they could wash up. Their horses had been groomed, fed, walked, and returned to the tether line. Since every man was on his own for breakfast, Tom and Caleb had to scrounge up something to eat.

John Cobb brought them some eggs he'd won playing cards. Cooked in fatback, they smelled delicious. With a bit of salt, they tasted even better.

Carter had them strike camp early. His small command now was nearly 100 men. They left Camp Dick Robinson and rode southeast for several hours, Tom and Caleb staying near the front of the column. New men usually rode near the rear after the first ride, so no one questioned the fact that the boys were told to ride behind the lieutenants.

Another militia led by Daniel Ellis, a wagonmaker, joined Carter. Ellis' command was a force almost equal to Carter's. Riding deeper into Tennessee, the ranks swelled to about 180 men. The third night, they camped with recruits for the Union Army south of Nashville and thirty-five miles east of Murfreesboro.

On the fourth morning after leaving Camp Dick Robinson, Carter and his two lieutenants approached Tom and Caleb. "Caleb, I've seen you shoot. Tell us honest, who shoots better? You or Tom?"

Tom answered, "It's always close, but Caleb's better. In three years, I only bested him six times, and I count those with two where I barely won."

"We're going out today or maybe tomorrow. John Hunt Morgan was around Murfreesboro and Reb cavalry's been crossing over from Alabama. Halleck cain't spare men from his advance on Corinth, so we got the job. Tom, you ride with Dan. Caleb's with Harrison."

When Tom went off to check on the horses he ran into John Cobb again and learned that Carter tended to stay near home, but that of late he'd been called on for special actions. Cobb told Tom that they were lucky they hadn't run into any bushwhackers. This far south of the Cumberland, secesh sentiments were inflamed by Yankee raids and the loss at Shiloh.

Before Tom walked away, Cobb told him to make sure that Caleb didn't get captured. The Rebs showed no mercy to niggers who'd kill whites.

Tom passed on what he heard to Caleb, who nodded. He knew what might happen, and he'd die before he'd let some rebel make a slave of him or worse. Still, he was jittery and didn't sleep well that night.

The fourth day passed without incident and so did most of the fifth. Riding into Bedford County, they spoke with a Unionist shopkeeper in Harrington, a few miles south of Murfreesboro. He'd been visited by Morgan just the week before.

"The man's a mere felon," the merchant said indignantly.

While they were talking with the merchant, one of Carter's scouts returned. Morgan was long gone he reported, but another group of bandits was only a few miles south. Ellis took his men on a route that swung out to the east. Carter let the scout take his command due south. His two lieutenants rode on either side of him. After a few minutes they dropped back.

Harrison said to Caleb, "We'll be north of the village. Carter'll drive 'em at us. The scout says we'll see the spot for the ambush. If they get by us, Ellis will be in place."

Once they got to the spot, Caleb knew what the scout had in mind. The horses could be hidden behind the ridge. From a position concealed by trees, Caleb and half the squad would have a clear shot at the head of the fleeing raiders. Harrison and the other half of the squad would be in a swale almost perpendicular to Caleb's position. They waited less than half an hour.

Caleb heard the gunfire, hoofbeats, and yells before he could see anything. He cocked the lever to put a round into the chamber and pointed the carbine toward the middle of the road. A cloud of dust suddenly appeared in front of him. He made out the lead rider. It was an easy shot, and he didn't wait for a signal to fire. The rider rolled lifelessly off his horse.

His second shot also found its mark before the column pulled up and the Rebs started to dismount. As they charged toward him, Harrison's line opened fire. Caught in a crossfire, the Rebels fired wildly in all directions. Some tried to remount their horses, but Carter's column came up on them from behind before they could escape. One rider stayed off to the side. When he drew his carbine up to his shoulder and fired, Caleb realized that it was Tom.

Tom shot three times in succession. Two shots hit one rider, but the third went wild. None of the Rebs paid him any attention. They were too focused on trying to escape. Tom ceased firing and so did Caleb. Finding the right target was too difficult in the melee. Harrison's men came out of the swale and charged toward the men, now in hand-to-hand fighting. They arrived in time to take prisoners.

Tom rode up to the encircled guerrillas. Caleb and the other half of Harrison's squad joined him. The engagement had lasted two or three minutes. Ten minutes later Ellis and his men rejoined Carter. Six of twenty-seven bushwhackers were dead, and eleven were wounded. Three of Carter's men were slightly wounded.

The prisoners were disarmed. Those able to ride had their hands tied behind them. Ellis walked over to two of the more severely wounded Rebs, hunkered down, and spoke to them for a minute. He called for one of his men, who also talked with the wounded men for several minutes, then walked away.

Ellis drew his pistol, aimed at the first man's head and fired. He repeated the process, killing the second man. Carter didn't even flinch. Tom and Caleb didn't dare ask what was happening, but Carter read their minds.

"They were going to die anyway," he said. "Kinfolk paid his respects afore they died."

The dead were placed in a line on one side of the road.

Carter saw that the Rebel wounded who were unable to ride were carried to a shady spot away from the road. Those who could ride were placed in a column guarded by Carter's men on each side.

"That was some good shooting," Harrison said to Caleb. "Your friend acquitted himself well, too. All these Rebs'll be standing trial."

Caleb was relieved to have his first battle over and done with. That night in camp, Tom told him what had happened earlier. Reb skirmishers saw Carter coming and rode into the village to warn their comrades.

Rebs had killed known Union sympathizers in the village. They were torching everything when the skirmishers came riding in. Seeing that they were outnumbered when Carter's men charged them, the bushwhackers skedaddled with a yell. Tom shot one, but didn't know if he'd killed or wounded him. Carter, Tom, and the rest of the group then chased the Rebs toward Caleb and the rest of Ellis' command who were waiting a mile outside of the village.

"How come the Rebs didn't see Carter's scout?" Caleb asked.

Tom shook his head and smiled grimly. "He got lucky. Got his information from a farm boy, who saw them riding in."

4

PERRYVILLE

After Carter's men delivered their prisoners to the Union garrison at Nashville, Carter's men dispersed into Carter County, leaving Tom and Caleb on their own. Carter brought them to his home, introducing them as new hired hands. No one asked questions.

The next week was quiet. Tom and Caleb made more ammunition. Pressing the primer caps in place was tedious and required great care. Measuring out the black powder required accuracy. Each load was weighed out twice before it was poured into the casing.

Fixing the ball was the next challenge. The slightly larger round had to be seated perfectly in the smaller casing. Having a less-than-airtight seal was asking for disaster. Once the lead bullet was firmly in the casing and level with the top ring, the crimp was used to make it absolutely straight.

It took three hours for each man to make forty bullets. At the end of the week (which had two rainy days when they couldn't work), they had 350 rounds apiece, including those brought from North Carolina. They each could carry only half

that many with them. The remainder would have to be left at
Carter's house.

They chased a lot of shadows that summer. News of great
battles and small reached them, but their own world was one of
local conflict. July 1862 saw battles at Memphis, Murfreesboro,
and Decatur, but the fights Tom and Caleb participated in bore
the names of little-known people and farms.

August brought the war closer. It began at Tazewell, where
Carter reluctantly rode with Tinker Dave again. Confederate
General Braxton Bragg was moving from Tennessee into Kentucky. He was a threat that had to be countered. Carter warned
the two Parkers that they could expect major action.

As Bragg's Confederate Heartland campaign began, the 6th
Kentucky Cavalry supported Union Colonel John DeCourcy,
who led the 16th Ohio. Colonel Reuben Mundy, who initially
had created the First Battalion of the 6th as his own independent battalion, called on the partisans of Carter and Tinker Dave
to assist DeCourcy and his Ohioans.

Mundy's Battalion had been in Union General Sam Carter's
brigade under General George Morgan's command in January
1862. Mundy was part of the expedition from Central Kentucky to capture the Cumberland Gap. The 16th Ohio and 49th
Indiana, commanded by Colonels DeCourcy and Ray respectively, also participated in this action.

They marched through London and Cumberland Ford, near
Pineville, and made their way near to the Gap. On February
14, Mundy's cavalry attacked the Rebels at the Gap, inflicted
substantial losses, and took some prisoners.

Sam Carter's force then moved in the direction of Big Creek
Gap on March 23. Cooperating with Union General Morgan's
other forces, Carter's men helped to take Cumberland Gap on
June 18, 1862. Mundy's battalion remained on duty in the area
of the Gap through most of July. The threat from Bragg brought
Mundy and DeCourcy south to protect the Union flank.

Because of Mundy's relationship with Carter's brother, the Reverend agreed to assist Mundy, in spite of Tinker Dave being part of the force. Carter brought his force, with Caleb and Tom, west to provide support for DeCourcy,

On August 6, 1862, DeCourcy's regiment fought an engagement with Confederate troops of the 3rd Tennessee under Colonel John C. Vaughn, near Tazewell. Carter's partisans fought on foot on the right flank. Tinker Dave and his men remained mounted in the rear as the 16th Ohio's reserve.

The 3rd Tennessee, from Colonel Vaughn to the lowest private in his command, wanted a real fight. Union loyalists, especially William Clift's 7th Tennessee, had been sniping at his men for months and harassed his march through Morgan and Scott counties. At Montgomery, fifteen of Clift's men were killed and seven taken prisoner. Vaughn lost seventeen men, five killed and twelve wounded.

Each force had a relative advantage. DeCourcy's Ohioans were better armed. Vaughn and his Confederates were equipped with many of the same weapons used by Carter and Beatty's Union partisans. Vaughn's rebel force, however, was substantially larger than DeCourcy's even with the reinforcements provided by Carter and Beatty.

When the fight began, it appeared that Vaughn was striking straight at the Union center. He committed only as many of his companies as he needed to lock the 16th Ohio in place. Vaughn held one company in reserve. Using the advantages of the terrain, the remainder of the Confederate 3rd Tennessee was concealed in the woods behind the gentle slope of a ridge.

Bill Carter and his men were in the unfortunate position of being near the crest on the reverse side of that ridge. When Vaughn's men emerged from the woods, they hesitated. They thought Carter's irregulars were another Confederate force. That notion was dispelled when Carter ordered his men to open fire.

Carter, seeing the size of the Rebel force, sent a courier to DeCourcy advising him of the unfolding situation that would flank the Union lines. Company G and H of the 16th Ohio, the only Union reserves, were sent to his aid. On his left, Company K fell back to refuse the right. It was not enough.

Caleb and Tom fired a full magazine each before having to fall back. At fifty yards, the 3rd Tennessee let loose the Rebel yell. The two Parker boys finished reloading and fired a few rounds, then joined the withdrawal. Company K was about to be overrun when Beatty and his sixty-five-man mounted force charged on horseback and fell on the Rebel left flank to stall their attack.

DeCourcy pulled his force back to reorganize the line. When Mundy and the First Battalion of the Union 6th Kentucky appeared, Vaughn broke off the attack. The 16th Ohio suffered three killed, twenty-three wounded. More than fifty were missing or captured. Vaughn and his Tennesseans saw nine killed and forty wounded. Beatty accounted for at least a dozen of those casualties.

The official report did not account for the losses among Carter's and Beatty's forces. John Cobb was among the wounded, two men were killed, and another six were missing. Beatty had fared slightly better, but none of his men were killed; four were wounded and only one was missing.

Mundy brought orders from Union General Morgan for Carter and Beatty. They were simple enough. Harass the Confederate rear and deny the Rebels support from any bushwhackers in the area. Morgan was specific about them staying to the east of the main Confederate force that was advancing into Kentucky.

A letter from Sam Carter to his brother supported the order and wished him godspeed. He added two specific cautions. The first reinforced Morgan's orders. Bill was to stay well east of the main Confederate force. In addition, any engagements with Rebel cavalry were to be avoided.

Bragg moved rapidly from Chattanooga through Franklin en route to Bowling Green. General Daniel Leadbetter, who had entered by way of Barboursville with 1,000 men, supported Bragg's invasion of Kentucky. Leadbetter had been given carte blanche to "break up Unionist activity, arrest their leaders, confiscate weapons, strip Scott County of supplies, and intimidate loyalists into submission."

Carter was the nominal head of the Unionist militia force, and Tinker Dave resented it. It was not surprising that he opposed Carter's proposed route. The compromise took them through Eagan and Jellico before crossing into Kentucky to turn north toward Barboursville. By shadowing Leadbetter, Beatty argued, the partisans could provide information on Confederate intentions. What they found was a trail of destruction.

South of Barboursville, they came upon a stand of trees along the road. There, they found thirty-four men in Union uniforms, who had been shot. In addition, there were thirteen men in civilian clothes, who had been hanged. Carter accounted for his six missing men from the engagement at Tazewell. Two of the remaining seven were identified as having ridden with Clift. A local man, who saw the executions, said that Confederate Colonel John Vaughn had issued the orders to kill the prisoners and traitors.

Vaughn, under Leadbetter's command, felt (as he later claimed) he would be "sustained in any course (he chose) to adopt" consistent with Leadbetter's instructions from Kirby Smith. The military and partisan prisoners were executed as an example to others disloyal to the Confederacy.

In response, Tinker Dave now felt justified in acting in like manner toward those supporting secession and the Confederacy. Carter objected. After he and Tinker Dave argued for more than half an hour, Tinker Dave withdrew his force in anger, leaving Carter with only sixty-three men. Two dozen of Carter's men then decided to join Beatty.

With only thirty-nine men, Carter knew he would be vulnerable to attack by bushwhackers. The Confederate army stood between him and the main Union force. He could either withdraw to Tennessee or take the risks that went with his orders from General Morgan.

Carter stood before the remaining men. "Y'all know I'm a preacher. I don't aim to preach," Carter began. The men shuffled their feet and looked at the ground. They figured that preaching was exactly what he was about to do.

"Cain't take the hunt outta the dog," a man near Tom muttered.

Carter ignored the comment. "All I plan to tell you is what I believe and why I'm going on," Carter continued. "There are two armies north of here. The men in those armies are gonna fight. Each man has his reasons, but I figger they come down to only a few."

He glanced at the faces of the men, trying to determine what he could say that would make them follow him. "One side believes they can abolish slavery and the other says they cain't. Another group wants to keep the Union together, but the secesh say no, they can leave. Lots of Tennessee and Kentucky men are divided that way."

"I suspect most of you, like them, are in it for a third reason, simply fighting to protect your homes and families. This is where we find our troubles."

"Ain't no trouble in keeping our wives and children safe," came a voice from inside the group.

"You're right," Carter answered, "if that's all there was to it. Tinker seems to think that protecting his home is an excuse for killing any man that disagrees with him. I don't."

A tall gaunt man, named Jim stepped forward. "None of them kilt back there were my kin. Coulda been though. If they were, I'd be riding with Tinker Dave."

Carter stared the man down. "If you did and you killed innocent folks, I'd disagree mightily. I fight for just two reasons. First, my brothers are with the Union army up there. I fight to protect my kin from bushwhackers. Second, and at this moment, I'm out here helping my brothers by helping the Army. It's a job I gotta do. Whyever y'all fight is yours to decide."

Jim spoke again. "Thought you was fighting to free the darkies."

"That, too," Carter replied, "but it's only a hope. For me, it ain't good enough reason to die. I'm going north. Who still rides with me?"

No one answered. Carter mounted his horse and so did all but three men. One of them was Jim. "Three dozen left," he thought to himself. "Back home, we'd be equally matched. Out here, Rebel cavalry and bushwhackers probably will outnumber us." He satisfied himself that they might survive.

Tom and Caleb rode at the back of the column. It was dusty and hard to breathe.

"I'm not sure about the Reverend," Caleb said.

"Me neither," Tom said. "You got a issue."

Caleb slowed his horse, and Tom matched him. They fell farther back. "Reverend Carter says he believes in abolition. He really don't care about colored folks any more than the slavers do."

"That why yore fighting?" Tom asked.

Caleb answered, "Got no other reason. If these Yankees don't care about our freedom, I'm fighting for my home. Thing is, home's a long way away, Tom."

"I respect that. Leastwise you got one more reason than I do. Not sure the so-called Union's worth saving. We both seen loyalists and secesh alike burn out families on either side."

Caleb hunched forward. "This war's just covering up feuds. Betcha it's the same back home. We don't need to stay here."

Tom leaned closer to Caleb. "For the moment we do. There's eighty mile a'tween here and Carter's house. It's more'n thrice that to Carolina."

The end of the column now was thirty yards ahead and was shielded by a stand of woods. They heard the sudden crackle of musket fire and the explosive sound of shotgun blasts. Caleb wheeled right and Tom followed. Their carbines were out as they entered the woods. Ten yards in, they saw the end of the Rebel lines. Dismounting, they tied their horses to a tree to advance on foot and under cover.

Caleb took aim and fired at one of the horse holders who grabbed his leg and fell screaming. The horses bolted. Tom did the same and four more horses ran off. Still, the bushwhackers were unaware of Caleb and Tom behind them. Taking advantage of the Rebel's ignorance, they both fired twice more. Two were killed, and the other two wounded.

Now Carter's men came pouring into the woods. Edging their way to the right, Tom and Caleb kept firing into the flank of the fleeing Rebel attackers. Several Rebels fired in their direction so quickly that their aim was poor. With a fairly clean line of fire almost always available to Tom and Caleb, it was a turkey shoot. As quickly as it began, it ended.

Carter came limping from behind. His horse had been shot out from under him. A bloody white rag on his left wrist showed that he also had been wounded. He carried his loaded Colt in his right hand. Tom thought it was Carter's wound that made him lean against a tree near a wounded horse holder. When he raised the Colt and fired, Tom was horrified. The man's head exploded with blood splattering in all directions. Carter limped another ten feet and repeated the act with another wounded

Rebel before turning around and returning to the road.

As Carter's men regrouped, the extent of the damage was assessed. Seven of Carter's men were dead and fifteen more were wounded. This included several men who had made the assault into the woods. "If you boys hadn't broken their flank, we'd a been slaughtered. With that open field over there, they'd a shot us standing or running. They musta thought there was more of us."

Three Rebels had escaped. Thirteen lay dead including the two wounded horse holders shot by Carter. Another eighteen were wounded. Carter killed them all. Tom and Caleb said nothing, but their resolve to leave Carter was strengthened.

Six of Carter's wounded men were unable to handle a hard ride. He had his own dead buried, and refused to leave his wounded behind. Gathering up as many supplies as the force could carry, using the horses they had captured, they moved into the mountains. A cave provided shelter safe from Confederate cavalry or guerrillas. Two days of rain covered any trail that the Rebels might use to find them.

Three of the seriously wounded men died over the next ten days. After two weeks, they were ready to ride again. Carter had lost most of the use of his left hand. Apparently several nerves had been severed. Carter's decimated force rode in Beatty's wake. At least they thought it was Beatty. The Confederate army apparently was well to the southwest around Bowling Green as the second week of September began.

Tinker Dave was burning and looting his way north in the direction of the Union garrison at Munfordville. Three Union regiments under Colonel John Wilder manned the fortifications that protected both the Louisville & Nashville Railroad station and the Green River Bridge. Tinker Dave was headed there in search of food, supplies, and ammunition. Without written orders, he was no more than a brigand on a rampage.

When Carter and his men arrived in Horse Cove on September 14, they heard news of the battle that was in progress. Confederate Brigadier General James Chalmers led the van of Bragg's Army of the Mississippi. His attack on the Union position under Wilder's command was being repulsed. The locals believed that a siege would begin the next day.

Carter had a different concern and a dilemma. While villagers were selling them food and supplies, he learned that the Rebel cavalry had passed through only hours before. Ammunition was not to be found, or at least none that anyone would part with.

Several options were discussed. One man suggested that Carter break up his forces and let them stay with local loyalists. This plan was rejected. If a Confederate sympathizer learned of their presence, Rebel cavalry or local guerrillas would sweep in and pick them off.

With the Munfordville garrison in danger of capture or forced surrender, the fort was not a safe haven. Union General Don Carlos Buell's Army of Ohio was too distant to rescue them. In addition, Carter and his men would have to ride in a wide arc to avoid an engagement with Confederate forces or guerrillas.

The Confederate advance had compelled Union General Morgan to give up Cumberland Gap and move across Eastern Kentucky to the Ohio River. Although Morgan broke up a band of guerrillas infesting that section, he also was too far away to offer safety.

Carter would not give up because of his orders from General Morgan. He chose to ride farther north. Strategically and tactically, it proved to be a sound decision. The siege of Munfordville lasted only two days. Colonel Wilder surrendered to Confederate Major General Simon Buckner on September 17 after seeing the size of the Rebel force while visiting the camp under a flag of truce.

At the time of Wilder's surrender, Carter's force was in temporary quarters east of Perryville and north of the Danville Pike. It had been a dry August and a drought-plagued summer. Carter was fortunate in finding a spring that provided adequate water for his men and horses.

This position allowed Carter and his partisans to attack Confederate supply trains. For ten days, as Bragg moved his 40,000-man army into position from Harrodsburg to west of Perryville and the Chaplin River, Tom and Caleb fought like secesh bushwhackers. Any attack that might last more than ten or fifteen minutes wasn't even attempted. The last two days they hit only one or two straggling wagons. Infantry or cavalry now heavily guarded the main wagon trains.

Rebel cavalry finally flushed Carter's force out on October 6. It was a quick skirmish, but two more men were killed and three of Carter's four wounded men were left behind. Tom took out three of the Rebs and was certain that at least one was dead. Caleb shot five of the bushwhackers. He wouldn't guess how many were dead. Tom said probably all of them were.

They had ridden hard for at least two hours before they stopped about a half-mile north of a large bend in the Chaplin River. Carter wouldn't let them build campfires. The firelight of the Confederate and Union forces was visible to the south and southwest from where they were situated. There was no sense doing something that might reveal their location.

On the morning of the 7th, they crossed the Chaplin River two miles north of the Confederate right flank. A long straight branch was cut and, for the first time, Carter flew the Stars and Stripes. Reaching the New Marketville Pike, they rode until stopped by Union General Phil Sheridan's rear guard.

Showing his orders from General Morgan, Carter asked to be taken to General Thomas. They were informed that the general, who had not yet arrived on the field, would be at the other end of the line. A small detachment of Union cavalry was sent with them. They camped at the southern end of the Union lines under the hospitality of General Charles Gilbert, who commanded the provisional Third Division.

General Thomas arrived with General Crittenden on the evening of October 7 in advance of their divisions. Crittenden's Division would form on Gilbert's right, and Thomas would bring his men into line overlapping the Lebanon Pike to extend the Union right flank about 11 A.M. on the 8th. Carter's men remained in camp behind Gilbert's position when Carter rode off to report to General Thomas.

Carter did not return until the morning of the 8th. On the evening of the 7th, he accompanied General Thomas back to hasten the advance of his division. Tom and Caleb remained with Gilbert's Division that morning as Confederate Generals Cheatham and Buckner attacked the Union left flank under the command of General Alexander McCook.

Buell urged McCook to push his brigades forward to meet the threat. Sheridan, trying to secure a source of water, advanced only as far forward as was needed to achieve that objective. Gilbert, in contrast, was urged to show restraint and kept his men behind their works. As a result, the Union left became disconnected from its center, leaving a large gap in the line.

Seeing the opportunity to collapse the Union left flank, Bragg ordered two brigades in Confederate General Anderson's Division forward and into the gap in the Union lines. They slipped through an unguarded ravine, and the fight progressed to a brawl of hand-to-hand warfare. Union Brigadiers Jackson and Terrill would be dead before the violently close combat ended. Buell, two miles in the rear, heard none of the battle.

Gilbert, meanwhile, continued to obey orders. He showed the required restraint. Bragg, however, smelling blood and a victory, sent forward Anderson's remaining brigade plus the divisions of Hardee and Cleburne. With the enemy coming straight at him, Gilbert had no choice but to react.

Gilbert's defensive line held. Tom and Caleb initially stood by, watching the elephant approach. They were slack-jawed. No battle they had seen compared to what was happening in front of them. Caleb focused on a single man furiously loading, firing, and reloading to fire again. He counted three and a half rounds per minute.

Caleb watched him take a bullet to the shoulder and fall screaming on the ground. Without thinking, Caleb stood up and ran the thirty yards to take the man's place in line. Using the breastworks to steady his aim, he fired first one round and then a second. He sensed Tom on his right. A quick glance confirmed his instinct. Caleb went back to work.

In five minutes, Tom and Caleb had expended sixty rounds of ammunition. Tom passed over the saddlebag he had the foresight to bring with him. "We better fire more slowly," Tom said with a grin. "There's already a purty big gap in the Rebel lines."

Caleb smiled back at Tom, "Shore enough. I'll pick my shots. See that sergeant?" He aimed at the man 100 yards ahead at the end of a regiment. Seconds later he fell.

The game of picking targets diverted them from the horrors around them. Rebel yell after Rebel yell cut through the sounds of battle, swelling above the rattle of musketry, exploding shells, and screams of wounded men. Tom and Caleb shut it all out. Making a competition of their deadly work allowed them to go back to their boyhood.

"Pretty good," Tom said as he took aim at a Rebel color bearer. "Watch this."

The man with the flag fell and so did the man who lunged to keep it from falling, thanks to Caleb.

Across the center and right of the Confederate line, the assault was stalling. Caleb stood back and Tom did likewise. They looked around to see dead and wounded men beside them. It was a scene of carnage. The wounded no longer screamed. Only low agonized moaning could be heard.

Some of the wounded were unconscious. Others were stirring or trying to get to their feet. Caleb felt a sense of shock at what he had done. He could not ignore his gory work. The rebels had made several charges at Gilbert's position. None had made it close enough to breach the line.

Crittenden and Thomas never engaged. Neither did the Rebel division under Johnson or Wheeler's cavalry corps. To reinforce the Union left, Gilbert had sent two brigades that enfiladed Buckner's exposed flanks and broke the Rebel attack. Finally, darkness came. McCook's Division had been pushed back more than a mile, but his line held. Sheridan anchored the Union left flank.

On the morning of the 9th, there was some skirmishing. Crittenden's First Brigade pursued skirmishers into the city, but they were the rearguard of Bragg's army that already was on the way back to Harrodsburg. Although Buell's Federals had suffered 4,211 casualties compared to 3,196 Confederate losses, the battle convinced Bragg to withdraw. Through McCook's stiff resistance, the Union had secured Kentucky for the duration of the war.

Of the original force, Carter returned with sixteen men plus himself. Tom and Caleb counted themselves among those few survivors. They had seen, felt, heard, and smelled more than they wanted to remember. Nothing heroic marked the experience. They knew only the relief of having survived.

The battle that Tom and Caleb fought paled next to the fighting to their left, where Terrill and his brigade had stood. There, the dead were laid out in rows for burial, bodies mutilated by cannon, torn apart by musket fire and by knife and bayonet wounds. The bodies were already bloating. In death

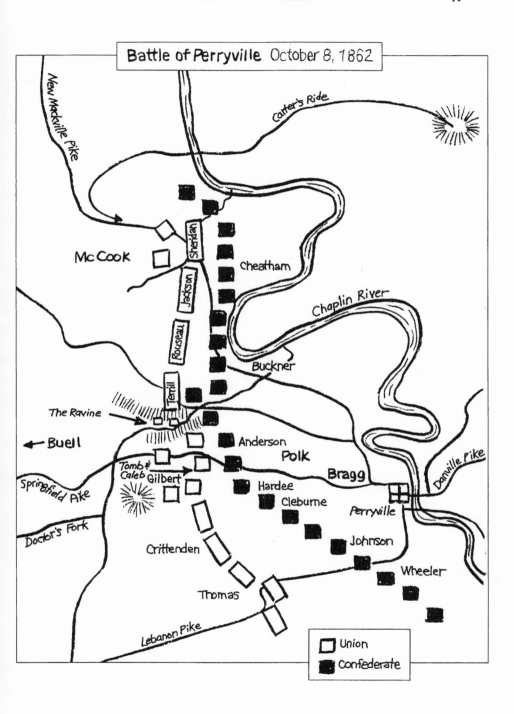

Battle of Perryville October 8, 1862

New Mackville Pike

Carter's Ride

McCook

Sheridan

Jackson

Rousseau

Terrill

Cheatham

Chaplin River

Buckner

The Ravine

Buell

Tomb of Caleb

Gilbert

Anderson

Polk

Bragg

Hardee

Cleburne

Perryville

Johnson

Danville Pike

Springfield Pike

Doctor's Fork

Crittenden

Thomas

Wheeler

Lebanon Pike

☐ Union
■ Confederate

they found commonality. The uniform no longer mattered.

Carter's partisans continued on with the Union cavalry to harass Bragg's rear as he withdrew into Tennessee. After they spent another three weeks in the saddle, General Thomas assured Carter that his orders were fulfilled.

5

HIGHLAND WINTER

Tom and Caleb returned to Carter's farm on Friday, November 7. Nothing had changed. Carter preached that Sunday morning. After their experience in Kentucky, Tom and Caleb found his sermon hollow. The Reverend had shown himself to be without mercy, and the difference between Tinker Dave and him was one of degree.

On Monday morning they sought Carter out, telling him they planned to leave in a week to spend time with their families. Carter reminded them of the danger and offered to give them a route to follow where they could find shelter.

They spent the next week replenishing their ammunition supply. Mrs. Carter prepared food for their trip. The Reverend worked with Tom and Caleb until they had memorized the way home. He told them that couriers would let people know that they were on their way into the area. Like their journey into eastern Tennessee, the trip home would be made mostly at night and through Confederate-held territory.

As they were leaving Tennessee near Soco Gap, Tom and Caleb met a column of Federal cavalry returning from a scouting trip. They quickly convinced the young lieutenant that they

rode with Billy Carter and escaped being shot. Tom explained
that they were traveling east because they were going home.
The lieutenant was skeptical, but a sergeant stepped in and said
that enough harm had been done without shooting any more
loyalists.

Instead of circling north into the mountains, their return
took them south and east before taking the mountain trails that
would lead them toward Waynesville. Carter had sent them that
way because Confederate cavalry were in the vicinity of western
North Carolina.

At a prearranged spot east of the mountains, they met one
of Captain Bryson's men. The people who were supposed to
shelter them would not let them stay in the house or on their
property. Instead, the boys were sent to a small shack that masked
the entrance to a cave.

Bryson's man, Seth, told them to quarter their horses inside
the cave. About a half a mile back was another entrance, but it
was too small for the horses. If they had to escape, it would be
on foot. That news didn't bother either of them because they
were only twenty-five miles from home.

Seth explained that Union cavalry had been through and
had destroyed the supplies needed by those still living in the
area. Confederate militia and companies of the 64th North Carolina had followed the Yankees and chased them out of the area.

Once the men of the 64th got close to home, however, they
began to desert. Seth warned Tom and Caleb to watch out for
these deserters, who would probably try to rob or kill them. He
also explained that the problem was made worse in several ways.
Loyalists, and Bryson was among them, had harassed the local
secesh as well as the 64th.

"We're all what they call vulnerable," Seth said. "Some Rebel
captain named Morris, who I don't know, said we was fierce,
vicious, and some word I didn't know. Claims the only way to
stop us is to be equally the same way."

Tom and Caleb nodded. Seth was angry. "This Captain Morris said we never gave him a fair fight, square up, face-to-face, horse-to-horse. Damnation, course we didn't. There was three time more a them than us. What in hell did he expect? 'Sides that, they knows this country well as we does. They couldn't even chase us good."

"Why not?" Tom asked innocently.

"Why not? 'Cause their deserters is jining with us. Almost all the 64th cavalry is Unionist now. Ol' Julius Gash, their captain is fit to be tied."

"So you're bushwhacking the Rebs here like we are in Tennessee and Kentuck?" Caleb asked.

"Sure enough, and burning their families out, too."

Tom thought for a moment. "Are the Rebs burning out loyalists?"

"Now you're at the heart of the matter. It's got real bad all over. Nobody's safe. Both sides is getting ready to ask Governor Vance to end it. Think that's a whistle in the wind, though. Everybody's filled up with hate now."

"How bad is it 'round Waynesville?" Tom asked.

Seth was lighting his pipe, so his answer was delayed. The look on his face telegraphed what he was about to say. "Bad enough. Not as bad as the Laurel Valley, though. Ain't been riding with Bryson lately. He's farther north round Jefferson and Sparta. New man, John Kirk, leading us now."

Caleb was getting anxious. "Any news from Waynesville?"

"Only thing I heard was that Union cavalry hit northwest of town. Few people got shot and hanged, but don't know who."

Caleb relaxed. At least they were *Union* soldiers. "When what was left of the 64th came up, they swung in from the east side," Seth continued. "Our men just rode out back into east Tennessee. Surprised you didn't pass by them."

"Fact is, we probably did. Damn fool lieutenant thought

we was Rebs. If Caleb hadn't told him about being with General Gilbert at Perryville and tangling with Vaughn at Tazewell, he mighta killed us then and there. Fact that Caleb's colored and fighting didn't hurt none neither."

Seth answered quickly, perhaps a little too quickly. "Don't rightly know that lieutenant personal. All I knows is he only had twenty-five men. They's supposed to be scouting and recruiting for new men."

That night they finished the last of Mrs. Carter's homemade biscuits, now stale, before continuing on. Riding through partial moonlight was slow going, in spite of their knowing the trail. They decided to risk riding the last ten miles in daylight, just to be done with it.

Choosing a trail through the deep woods, they approached from the north side, over the top of the mountain behind the homestead. None of the sounds of the blacksmith's shops greeted them. In the brisk fall air, the sound of the hammer on metal usually carried for a long distance.

They silently rode down the last slope until Caleb's brother, George, saw them. He ran at them with a holler. "Ma! Ma! They's back!" Caleb hushed him. Who knew who might be around?

Sissy and Melinda came out the door of one house. Annie Lee and Maggy burst from inside the other house. Tom spotted his mother down by the chicken coop.

"Where's Pa? Where's John?" Caleb asked before Susan reached them. Caleb saw the tears in his mother's eyes.

"Let's go in," Sissy said in a strained voice. "We'll tell you."

Once inside Susan's house, the girls hugged their brothers, tears streaming down their faces.

"What the hell happened?" Tom demanded.

"Watch your mouth, boy." Susan followed them through the door. Her eyes were sad, but her tone angry. "Plain and simple, your pa's dead. Killed by damn Yankees." Her voice rose. "And the two of you off killing our own people."

Caleb plopped down into the chair behind him. Tom caught himself against the stonewall of the kitchen hearth. Both were too stunned to speak.

Susan looked straight at Tom. "Your father was a Union man. I only agreed halfway with him. Neither of us wanted slavery. Lord knows I couldn't. Sissy and her kids are kin to me. Protecting ourselves is another matter."

Tom started to speak, but Susan wouldn't let him. "Your Pa and Jonah hid every stray dog came through here. Didn't matter if he's Confederate nor Yankee, deserter or loyal to his side. They was good men. Then that lieutenant and two dozen of his Yankees comes up here looking for recruits."

"Think I know who you mean, Ma."

"If you didn't shoot them, you lost a great chance. John wouldn't tell them anything one way or the other. They shot Jonah where he stood. The man hadn't said a word. 'Twas pure meanness."

"What about Pa?" Tom asked.

Susan's emotions overcame her. She sat down and closed her eyes. Maggy stroked her mother's arm. Susan opened her eyes and shrugged off her daughter's touch. "They hanged him," she said without expression. "Not once, but five times. Every time he passed out, they'd bring him back. Every time, he wouldn't tell them nothing. Last time, he was gone for good. After stealing our food, the damn Yankees just rode off and left him dead on the ground."

Tom didn't speak. He walked to the doorway. Caleb followed him through the door. Together, they went to the graveyard down the hill on the far side of the blacksmith shop. The two sons stood by their father's graves. Their tears were silent and bitter.

After some time, they heard George beside them. "I want to go with you," he said.

"You're staying here, boy," Caleb said. "Someone's gotta watch over the families. Tom and me has work to do. If we don't come back, the work is yours to do."

"But I don't know enough," George replied.

"Then we'll teach you afore we leave," Caleb said with finality.

Tom followed Caleb back to the horses. Silently they unsaddled them.

Dinner was somber, silent. Abruptly Melinda burst out, "They're dead. So what do you boys do now? Keep fighting?"

After a moment Tom replied, "I'll stay here through the winter and help Caleb and George. After that, I'm going east to jine Lee's army."

"You ain't going by yourself," Caleb said.

Tom gave Caleb a questioning look, "You gonna fight for a country believes in slavery?"

"There weren't no slaves in the United States? Tinker Dave treat nigrahs any better then the secesh does? Yankees killed my Pa, too. I cain't fight with Carter no more. We both seen what he does."

"So when do we go?" Tom asked.

Sissy interrupted, "It's all right for folks to know you're here, Caleb. Ain't true for Tom. He's gotta stay hid."

"That's right," Susan added. "Jonah built a dry cellar 'neath their house. You'll have to stay there. It'll be cold this winter."

"If anyone asks about Tom, we can say he's still fighting out west," Caleb said.

Tom was indignant, "I gotta help out. There's things I can do inside."

"Long's you stay inside when people is about, that's fine. Otherwise, you're inside," Susan said.

"It's done, then," Sissy said. "But you ain't sleeping in this house til you get rid of those lice."

After dinner, water was set to boiling. The boys would have to clean up outside in the chilly night air. Once Tom got in the tub, George and Caleb ferried the water. George combed through Tom's hair over and over until there was no sign of lice. Then, his head was washed several times with lye soap. He howled as the final rinses of alcohol were poured onto his scalp. Caleb was next and he howled louder than Tom.

The women burned their clothes. "No sense washing them," said Sissy with resignation. Only their hats were spared after Susan dipped them in boiling water then dried them over a smoky fire. Satisfied that the boys were lice-free and her house was safe from vermin, she let them back in for the night.

Fall gave way to winter. Tom built wheel rims and guns. Caleb taught George until his skills were good enough to keep the business going. There were the expected questions about Tom and why Caleb had come back without him, but most people seemed to accept the simple explanation that Caleb was here to keep the business going. With the shortage of black-smiths and any other kind of tradesmen, customers seemed more grateful than concerned about Tom's whereabouts.

Susan, Sissy, and their daughters had brought in the harvest almost alone. Tom objected, but none of them would let him go where someone might detect his presence. A few Confeder-ate deserters and escaped Union prisoners came up to the house. They were trying to reach Tennessee. Susan gave them what food she could spare and sent them on their way. In every re-spect, the family tried to make things appear normal.

As Christmas approached, the need for blacksmithing ser-vices declined. The household turned its efforts to preparing for the winter. Caleb provided game that was smoked and put up for the winter. Game was scarce. Men hiding in the hills had reduced the number of deer, pheasant, and wild turkey. The women finished canning and drying apples, beans, and other foods for the winter.

On Christmas Day they celebrated the Confederate victory at Fredericksburg twelve days earlier. John Hunt Morgan's success at Hartsville, Tennessee, including the capture of 1,800 Yankees, three weeks before Christmas added to their good cheer. The Parker household now was decidedly pro-Confederate. Their loyalty, however, had more to do with two empty chairs than a belief in any cause. Espousing a belief in secession kept the few remaining Unionists in the county away from their home.

Susan and Sissy loaded the wagon on Christmas afternoon. They had put aside food to share with Confederate widows and women who still struggled, with only meager assistance from the North Carolina and Confederate governments.

"We may not be wealthy," Susan said, "but there's worse off than us. Caleb, maybe you could help to fix things. With so many of the men gone, there's a real need."

"We can't afford to give our work away," said Tom. "There ain't enough left for us."

Susan and Sissy exchanged glances. "We have plenty," Susan said. "John and Jonah used Confederate script when they had to. They kept Federal dollars and coinage. We got it hid. You and Caleb need to see where."

Caleb and Tom followed their mothers to more than a dozen spots around the farm. The money was under the floor boards, in hidden compartments, and buried under the water barrels. "There's cut rials in the old cellars," Sissy said.

Gold and silver would buy almost anything. Confederate currency had questionable value, even at that point. Tom and Caleb were satisfied that the family would be financially secure—as long as raiders didn't find the cache.

Anti-Union feelings were inflamed shortly after the new year began. On January 8, John Kirk with fifty Unionists, plus deserters from the 64th North Carolina, made a raid from Shelton Laurel to Marshall to get salt, supplies, and foodstuffs that they needed for the winter. Like most everyone else in the highlands, they were in a desperate way. Salt, in particular, was needed for curing and preserving meats and hides.

Kirk's men stole everything that was left among the few stores in the town. Then, Kirk made a critical mistake. He ransacked the home of Colonel Lawrence Allen on Main Street. Allen's wife and three sick children were harassed. The men even stole the children's blankets off their beds.

Allen and James Keith had formed the 64th North Carolina in Madison County where Marshall was located. They quickly put together 250 Confederates under their authority from General Henry Heth, the Commander of the Department of East Tennessee. Allen moved his force up the Laurel Valley to Marshall. Once there, he learned that his son had died and one of his daughters was likely to die shortly.

Incensed, Allen went on a rampage. Keith, coming in from the north, located fifteen men and boys who were purported to be among the raiders. Perhaps only five actually were participants. All but two, who escaped, were summarily executed. All thirteen were related to each other, and seven of them were Sheltons. The oldest was sixty-five and the youngest twelve. Confederates Allen and Keith showed no more mercy than was shown by Kirk and his Yankees.

Unionists called this the Shelton Laurel Massacre. Confederate loyalists called it justice. The Parkers, and particularly Tom and Caleb, saw it as the so-called warfare they had witnessed in Tennessee and Kentucky. It wasn't war. It was a local feud borne of hunger, frustration, and unrelated hatreds brought to fruition. The act of war was only an excuse.

Early January also brought mixed news about the war and Federal initiatives. Confederate General Braxton Bragg had withdrawn from Murfreesboro, Tennessee, after fierce fighting at Stone's River. Bedford Forrest and John Hunt Morgan had returned from successful forays into Union-held territory.

Lincoln's Emancipation Proclamation freeing the slaves confirmed southern beliefs that the Yankee government had less interest in preserving the Union than in dominating the South. Unionists in western North Carolina lost much of their interest in the northern cause. Only the abolitionists in the highlands remained opposed to Confederate aims, and they kept silent. Unionist support was in complete decline. It would be late 1864 before pro-Union sentiments would reappear.

Tom was anxious to leave. Caleb promised that they could be headed east at the end of March. George's apprenticeship would be finished then. Tom was unsatisfied, but he agreed to wait until spring.

Tom was concerned about transporting their horses on the train. There was the risk of their being confiscated by some quartermaster or being stolen by Union or Confederate bushwhackers. Caleb was more concerned about being delayed by questions about who they were and where they had been. Neither concern proved realistic.

The initial plan was to ride north, staying in the mountains for as long as possible before turning east. Somewhere before Danville, they would board the train and go to Richmond. News of Union activity in the upper Shenandoah Valley changed their plans. Their new route took them entirely by horseback into the Piedmont and then north through Petersburg.

South of Petersburg they saw a young black boy sitting by the side of the road. He was wearing nothing more than a sack with arm and neck holes.

"Whatchyer name, boy?" Caleb asked. The boy just stared at them. Caleb asked again. Still no answer.

"Maybe he's deaf," Tom offered. "Leave 'em be."

"Not deaf," the boy said.

"Then, whatchyer name, boy?" Caleb asked a third time.

"Why you wanna know?"

"Usually it's sociable," Tom said.

The boy stood up. "They calls me Jamie. Whatchyer names?"

Tom and Caleb introduced themselves. Jamie looked to be about twelve. He actually proved to be fourteen.

"Where y'all going to?" Jamie asked.

Caleb smiled. "Jine Lee's army."

Jamie smiled back, "Why you do that?"

Tom was amused by the boy's apparent innocence. He stood just watching and listening. Caleb asked, "You a slave?"

"Used to be," Jamie replied

Skeptical of the boy's answer, Caleb asked, "Used to be?"

"Master's dead. Mistress, too. All dead. Yankee cavalry burned everything down to the ground. We all just ran off. I'm looking for work," Jamie answered.

"Reckon you can work for us," Tom said. "Food and two dollar a month."

Caleb added, "You need proper pants and a shirt. Shoes, too, if you want. From now on, though, you're my brother. Fewer questions."

"Don't want no shoes. Hurts my feet. I'll work for you though, Caleb," he said, acknowledging Caleb's plan.

Caleb reached out his hand. "Come on, ride with me."

Jamie shook his head as if to say no. "Wait," he said and then he ran in the direction of the woods. A few minutes later, he came trotting out on an old horse. "Been saving her to sell if I had to," Jamie said with pleasure. "Now I won't slow y'all any."

6

CHANCELLORSVILLE

Jamie found pants, shirt, and an old hat in Petersburg. He was glad to be dressed like a boy with "real clothes." Continuing north, they arrived in Richmond on April 30. Finding no place to stay, they continued out of the city. They learned that both armies were in the vicinity of Fredericksburg.

The Yankees were north of the Rappahannock River. Union cavalry were reported northwest, near Hanover Junction and Ashland. Tom suggested that they ride northeast and swing back to approach Lee's army, which was west of Fredericksburg. He saw no reason to risk being captured before they even had a chance to fight. Caleb agreed.

They crossed the Pamunkey River and continued north until they reached the Mattapony River. Turning northwest and staying on the south bank of the Mattapony, they rode past Guiney Station and Spotsylvania Court House. Their westward turn around Spotsylvania Court House took them beyond the Confederate army.

A local farmer sent them east on the Orange Plank Road. "Make sure you turn south on the Brock Road, or you'll walk straight into the Yankee lines," he said. "Heard that Hooker crossed the Rapidan and Rappahannock yesterday."

Tom thanked the man. They wheeled their horses toward the road and took off at a trot. It already was early afternoon. As they rode, they thought they could hear the sounds of men marching. Sheltered by the dense forest, they could see nothing.

"That's either Yankees coming straight at us or Lee's retreating. Folks in Richmond said the Federals had twice as many men as Lee," Tom said.

"Reckon we'll find out soon enough," Caleb said casually.

Jamie rode quietly behind them. Tom unholstered his pistol. Seeing that it was loaded, he put it back in place. He then checked his carbine. Caleb did the same. Both left their carbines out and resting across their saddles.

"Y'all fit afore?" Jamie asked.

Caleb turned and looked back at the boy. "Out west. We was at Perryville and Tazewell. Nothing like the big battles here in Virginia and Maryland, though."

"You ever see a battle, Jamie?" Tom asked.

"No, sir."

"Stay with us, and you will," Caleb added. "We're gonna keep you outta it. You just get to watch. Hush now, 'til we find out who's ahead."

They slowed their horses to a walk as the road turned gently to the east. Ahead was a column of Confederate soldiers marching north on the Brock Road. "Don't look like a retreat to me," Tom said.

It wasn't much of a road. It was more like a wide trail. Tom, Caleb, and Jamie were three abreast facing it. Looking up and down the road, all they could see was a continuous line of Rebel troops. Taking advantage of a break in the column, they fell into the line of march.

A captain stepped up beside them. "What unit you with?"

he asked Tom pointedly.

"We ain't yet, sir. Looking to jine up. What unit's this?"

"This here's the 23rd Virginia, Company H. We're known as the Richmond Sharpshooters. I'm Captain Tompkins, Rob Tompkins. Who're you?"

"Name's Tom Parker. This here's Caleb and his brother Jamie."

"They yours?" Captain Thompkins asked.

Tom looked at Caleb who just nodded. "Nope. Both free. Caleb and me was fighting with militia out west. Not much of a war. Reckoned we'd try our hand with Lee."

"Y'all kin fight with us today," Tompkins offered, "but the boy will have to stay behind. Your carbines'll do. Y'all got at least sixty rounds?"

Caleb said, "We got more than that. Jamie'll watch our horses. Y'all going into a fight anytime soon?"

Tompkins was taken by surprise. "Most certainly are, boys. Probably less than two hours."

"Guess our timing was good," Tom interjected. "We're ready."

"Stay here in line. When we get there, send the boy up the pike. You can get him later." With that, Tompkins smiled, slowed his pace, and rejoined his company.

Another mile ahead they crossed the Germanna Plank Road. After another three-quarters of a mile, Company H reached the Chancellorsville Turnpike. It was twenty minutes before the regiment was deployed.

Jamie was told to care for the horses and sent back up the road. Tom and Caleb were in the second line of the regiment's front, which extended about seventy-five yards. They were placed near the line closers because no one knew how they might perform under fire. When everyone was in place the brigade advanced to take its place in the overall formation.

As they traveled up the road, Caleb thought he saw other colored troops among the company in front of them. He wasn't sure though. When the regiment deployed, however, he could see more clearly. He started counting the colored soldiers and stopped at fourteen. "I must talk with some of them," he thought. "Why are they here?"

The 23rd Virginia, as part of Warren's Brigade, Colston's Division, was placed directly across the Turnpike. Doles' and O'Neal's brigades were in front of them. Although they didn't know it at the time, they were more than a half-mile from Union General Howard's XI Corps.

At around 6 P.M., the order came to move forward. They were off the road and in the underbrush. It was thick with brambles and thorns that tore at their clothes. The rope-strong catbriers were worst of all. Tom put on the gauntlets he'd bought in Tennessee to protect his hands. Caleb did the same. The men beside them eyed their covered hands enviously.

The advance was slow and tedious. In front of them, rabbit, deer, and a lone fox scuttled frantically to get out of their way. Several men stumbled and fell. They were back on their feet quickly with bloody and dirt-covered hands.

About a quarter-mile later, they started up a gentle slope. At the crest of the slope, the pickets were pulled in. They were still nearly a quarter-mile from the Union flank. The pace quickened as they advanced another 150 yards.

First came the explosion of the cannon firing down the turnpike. Then came the deafening Rebel yell from Doles' and O'Neal's brigades. "*Yyyeae-ooohhhe! Yyyeae-ooohhhe!*" Part scream, part whistle, fully ululation, it pierced the sky and the ears. The sound was hostile and filled with revenge.

It was a sound ever so sweet to Tom and Caleb. Their voices joined the chorus. Uncontrolled, their feet hurled them forward toward the panicked Yankees on the other side of the field. Pickets from the 45th New York fired at the Rebel line surging

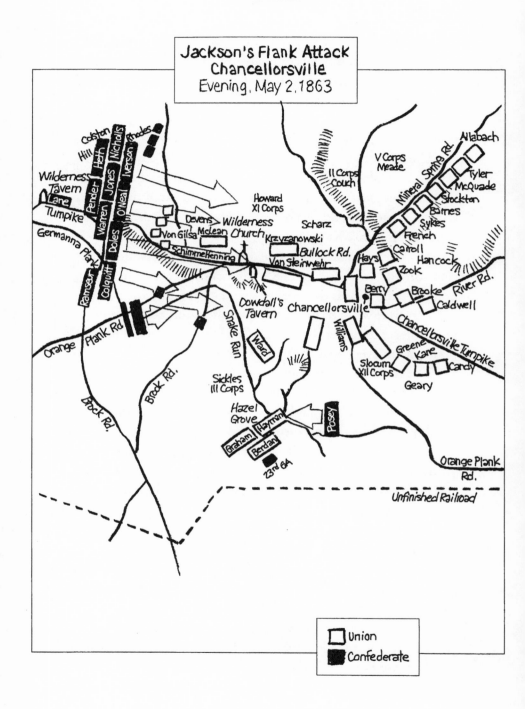

at them. The bullets whizzed harmlessly over their heads.

Tom and Caleb were in a footrace and passed through the first line. They overtook the men of the regiment in front of them. Caleb looked back. He couldn't see the corporal, who had been the line closer on his right. Tom had screamed himself hoarse. Caleb realized that he had also. His throat was burning.

A color-bearer had scrambled over a crude abatis. Caleb followed him. Tom, in turn, followed Caleb. A few Yankees were trying to stop the gray tidal wave, but it was an irresistible force. Caleb saw a Yankee raise his rifle to his shoulder. In a smooth, swift action, he pulled the carbine to his shoulder and fired. The Yankee fell as his rifle fired into the air to no effect.

Tom fired immediately after Caleb and a Yankee sergeant fell. He dearly loved shooting sergeants and searched them out among the enemy lines. They cocked their carbines to put another round in the chamber. Looking to see the movement of the battle, they turned right and followed the mass of men to the southeast. To their front was the 25th Ohio, which fired a full volley at the approaching Rebels.

A return volley from the Rebels was answered by another from the Ohioans. Again the rebels fired. The 25th Ohio fell back and joined the 75th. Doles' men plus others from Warren's brigade, which now included Tom and Caleb, were not to be easily repulsed. They were firing downhill at the 25th and 75th, which were behind cover in the underbrush.

As Caleb moved foward, a colored soldier in front of him slipped and fell. Caleb came up beside him as the man scrambled to his feet. "You free?" he yelled.

The black man looked back at him in amazement. "Course I am. Slaves cain't fight." Caleb smiled and before he could turn away, the man added, "You as crazy a nigger as me." Then they continued on their own ways.

Cannon had followed them up the pike. Now, these cannon supported the infantry's advance. Canister and grape swept the Union lines. As they had at Perryville, Tom and Caleb picked their targets. The smoke hung thick in the air, however, and they soon could see nothing more than muzzle flashes.

As they knelt to get under the smoke layer, the Federals fired another volley. Tom felt a bullet tear a gash near a rib on his right side. It continued on its path through the back of his coat. Caleb was grazed by a bullet that nicked his neck near his left shoulder. Neither was wounded seriously or bleeding heavily. They would tend to their injuries only when the day's batttle was over. What they now knew was that the Yankees were firing low.

The man on Caleb's right was hit in the groin near his left hip. He spun around and hit the ground screaming in pain. The man on Tom's left took a bullet in the stomach that threw him to the ground, flat on his back. He was graced by unconsciousness as he bled to death where he lay.

Again they began to pick their targets. Tom fired at a man standing in the open. He saw the blood explode from beneath the soldier's belt buckle. As the man fell to his knees, Tom could see the agony on his face.

The effects of the concentrated Rebel fire broke the Federal line before he could squeeze off a second round. Again, they were in pursuit of the fleeing Yankees. A Confederate captain came riding up the line on horseback. He stopped near Tom and Caleb waving his sword and urging the men to press their pursuit.

Tom rushed in the direction of the man he had just shot. When he reached him, the man was on his back staring uncomprehendingly at the sky. Blood soaked the hands that clutched his abdomen as well as his pale blue pants and dark blue jacket. The man coughed and sprayed more blood into the air.

"Kill me," he pleaded.

Caleb looked at Tom. "He'll die anyway. Don't waste the bullet."

"It'll be slow," Tom replied as he casually raised the carbine to his shoulder.

The man closed his eyes. Tom fired directly at his chest after which the man's whole body relaxed. His hands were lying neatly in his lap. He was dead. Tom and Caleb moved on.

Across the depression, about twenty-five yards away, were a Union officer and a sole enlisted man. The officer had his hands cupped to make himself heard as he screamed orders. The enlisted man had a pistol. He pointed it at the Confederate captain. The muzzle flashed.

He fired five times and missed each time. Tom and Caleb turned to fire at him. Both he and the Yankee officer disappeared into the brush. One reappeared two minutes later apparently unhurt, fifteen yards farther away.

The chase continued. A Confederate soldier yelled, "It's a skedaddle! Lookit them run!" When they overran the second knot of resistance from the Ohioans, they found the officer who had been screaming the orders, dead. A single shot had pierced his heart.

Crossing the crest of the slope on the other side of the depression, Tom and Caleb saw Union artillery 120 yards in front of them. The artillery opened fire placing solid shot and explosive shell all along the line. Men were sent sailing into the air. Others were simply torn apart. Their second round was canister.

The balls ripped off limbs, leaving ragged stumps and disgorging blood and tossing flesh all over. Other pieces opened large wounds in the body or destroyed faces. Men fell in clumps screaming or dead and silent. Those left standing were enraged, and the audacity of the artillery only strengthened the Confederate resolve.

They rushed the cannon. Its infantry support broke and ran. They were eighty yards from capturing the cannon when they limbered up and left the field chasing after their own infantry. Tom and Caleb continued toward the position abandoned by the Union guns. They stopped at the crest and looked across the field at the fleeing men of the shattered XI Corps. "Looks like a horse stampede," Caleb observed. "Two-legged horses that is." Caleb was grinning.

"Forward, men, forward! Press forward!" said a firm voice from behind them. The men turned to see who was ordering them on. It was Jackson. His eyes were clear and blue. He was sitting relaxed on Little Sorrell, but the intensity, the battle fever, was on him. The men started to cheer. "No, men," he said. "Press on! Press on!"

The men turned and again began the pursuit. "I'll be damned," another soldier said. "Ole' Blue Light, hisself." They crossed the field. Tom looked behind him. Jackson was gone. He had ridden off to spur on the troops on another part of the battlefield.

Bunched up in the tangled underbrush on the other side of the field, Tom, Caleb, and the others found clusters of Yankees jumbled together and frozen with fear. "No shoot us!" they called out with German accents as their hands went into the air over their heads.

The temptation to kill them was strong. Tom raised his carbine to his shoulder. "No, Tom," Caleb said, "we're better'n that. No sense being like the Reverend."

Tom remained in firing position. His breathing was ragged. Slowly he lowered the gun, and then raised it again as if he had changed his mind. Finally, he lowered it entirely. "I cain't be a coward. It'd be like shooting fish in a barrel."

All around the surrounded prisoners, the Rebels danced and whirled about in wild enthusiasm. Many fired their guns in the air. The captured Germans couldn't understand a word that was being said. Watching the scene in front of them only increased their fear. A few fell to the ground face down, still pleading not to be killed.

The Confederate officers struggled to maintain order and to continue pressing the attack forward. Many of the men were hungry and thirsty after the long countermarch. They stopped only long enough to loot the Yankee camps of their supper. Once fed, however incompletely, they were ready to continue.

Doles' advance had hardly slowed at all. Ahead of Jackson's forces, the retreat of the XI Corps had become a reckless mass of men, horses, wagons, and cannon. Oliver O. Howard, the Union general responsible for the XI Corps, later would report that there was "blind panic and great confusion."

At the time, Howard was shaken and thinking only of his professional future. "I'm ruined! I'm ruined! I'll shoot if you don't stop. I'm ruined! I'm ruined!" he cried as he attempted to rally his shattered corps.

Tom and Caleb continued their pursuit with the Georgians. They were completely separated from the 23rd Virginia and were once again in thick forests. A mile east of Wilderness Church, they encountered resistance again, but from an unexpected opponent. It was the 8th Pennsylvania Cavalry.

The charge came straight down the Turnpike. Seeing that the Confederates were too tightly massed, the cavalry veered left and directly at Doles' men. Tom and Caleb heard yells and hoofbeats. Marching in the third line back, they saw the cavalrymen trampling over the skirmishers and then slashing through the first line.

The boys had time to prepare, unlike those in the first two lines who took the initial brunt of the attack. Believing that the entire Yankee cavalry was charging, some of these men tried to surrender. The third and fourth line, however, saw the tenuous position of the Yankees more clearly.

They fired a concentrated volley straight at the horsemen. Caleb fired at the sword arm of the cavalryman bearing down on him. It was the only available target as his horse's head shielded the man's body. Tom aimed at the horse's chest.

Horses stumbled in front of the third line throwing their riders over their heads. The bodies were flung into the trunks of trees and among Doles' men. Other cavalrymen were struck by multiple shots that lifted them out of their saddles and onto the ground in the path of the horses behind them.

Their carbines allowed Caleb and Tom to quickly place another round in the chamber. The remaining infantry needed fifteen seconds to reload. It was barely enough time. A second battalion of Union cavalry was charging over their living and dead comrades. Those Confederates who had reloaded fired.

The charge was broken. What cavalry remained turned back. Jackson's advance continued. The Georgians tried to bring their ragged line back into order. Caleb approached a wounded Yankee corporal who was struggling to reach his pistol. As he kicked it out of reach, Caleb went to shoot him. A saber suddenly appeared from behind him that was thrust upward from the man's stomach and into his chest cavity.

The death was almost instant. A gurgle from the corporal's throat was followed by a spurt of blood and bile from the man's mouth. Then, it was over. His eyes, however, stared straight at Caleb. It was a look of absolute incredulity.

"Better the men see me kill 'em than you," the lieutenant with the saber said grimly before shouting an order for the men to form up.

Tom looked at Caleb and said. "Guess he's a little touchy about coloreds killing whites." Caleb just nodded.

Once past the cavalry, the Georgians moved on, turned slightly southeast, and quickly reached the heights at Hazel

Grove. One company encountered a small Yankee battery that fled at the approaching wave of gray. A cannon and two caissons were abandoned. The attack now swung right and into the positions left vacant by Sickles' Third Corps.

They were behind the Federal lines with a group of men from at least six different regiments. In front of them was more abandoned equipment including stacked rifles, caissons, supply wagons, ambulances, and mobile forges. Tom and Caleb were taken by the quality of these forges. They were better than any they had ever worked. "Imagine what we could do with those," Caleb said.

Tom replied, "Wouldn'tcha love to take one home?"

"Sure would," answered Caleb. "This battle's 'bout done with it getting so dark. Still don't see how we'd haul it outta here." His words were nearly drowned out by the cannon fire from the other side of Hazel Grove. Pieces of dirt and clumps of grass flew up in the air in front of them. "More canister!" Caleb hollered.

In the dim light, they could barely make out the figures on the other side. "That's gotta be the rest a the Yankee army," Tom said. The order came to fire. On command two volleys were directed across Hazel Grove. More cannon fire followed for fifteen continuous minutes.

Colonel Winn, of the 4th Georgia, who was leading this small group on Doles' right flank, ordered their withdrawal. Winn was satisfied that his men could move no farther forward until dawn. He ordered the men back into the lines.

"Think we should find the 23rd?" Tom asked Caleb.

"We rightly should. Them Richmond Sharpshooters made the offer."

"But we fought with these Georgia boys."

"Didn't make no difference this time," Caleb said. "We was with friends and that's all that counted. Now, though, we should find them or some North Carolina men."

"I'd druther the Virginians," Tom said.

"Good enough."

It took them two hours to find the 23rd Virginia. On the way, they heard various rumors that Jackson had been killed. Not knowing what to believe, Tom and Caleb ignored them.

Men Tom didn't know hugged him joyously. Caleb stood by on the side, smiling at Tom's confusion and discomfort. The men were too exhausted to celebrate long. Despite their concerns about Jackson, they soon fell asleep on the ground.

Caleb, however, did not allow himself the luxury of rest. He couldn't find Jamie or the horses. It occurred to him that there were no horses anywhere. "Everybody walking. Horse-holders ain't here yet," one soldier said. "You lost your massuh, boy?"

The soldier noticed the carbine in his hand and looked away. Caleb ignored the question. He started to wander westward on the Turnpike. Seeing the rows of soldiers through which he must pass, he thought better of it. He sat down by the campfire and sipped at a cup of chicory-laced coffee. Sleeping soldiers nearby snored.

"Looking for something?" Roused from his drowsiness, Caleb turned around to see Jamie standing behind him.

"Where's the horses?" Caleb asked.

"Over yonder. They's groomed and fed. Got them some oats, too."

"How'd you do that, boy?"

"Told 'em you an Tom's scouts for the 23rd."

Caleb reached over for his blanket. "Come on, boy. Now we both kin get some sleep." Jamie walked over and lay down beside Caleb, who pulled the blanket over both of them. In moments, they were both asleep.

7

INVASION!

Sporadic Yankee cannon fire broke through their sleep. Three hours later they were awakened and told to break camp. The rumors about General Jackson appeared to be true. No one knew the details. Captain Tompkins was the only one they believed.

Tompkins formed the company in a column of three amid the rubble of the abandoned Yankee camps. He ordered them to face left and began, "I've spoken with Colonel Walton. We'll be going about half a mile forward. There have been several changes in command. Colonel Warren was wounded. Colonel Williams is now in charge of the brigade. Major Wood has taken Colonel Williams' place leading the 37th Virginia."

"What news of Jackson?" someone called out from the ranks.

Everyone waited in silence. "In the darkness and confusion," said Tompkins, his voice strained, "General Jackson was wounded. The 18th North Carolina fired at him and his staff. They thought that the general's party was Yankee cavalry."

The same voice called out again, "Is he alive?"

Tompkins did not hesitate. "Yes, and they think he'll be fine. He'll probably lose an arm. General Stuart assumed command of the corps. General Lee has ordered him to press the attack at daylight."

An aide said something inaudible. Tompkins looked up and down the ranks. "There's a new man here. Think his name is Tom. Has his nigger and his boy with him," he said.

Tom answered, "Right here, Cap'n. The nigrah's name's Caleb."

"You boys are mounted and have carbines. Y'all don't belong in the line. Colonel Walton wants you as couriers. Mount up and report to the regiment," Tompkins said.

Tom and Caleb replied, "Yes, sir," in unison and left the ranks to find Jamie and the horses. Jamie had the horses saddled and ready.

"Either you got good sense or you're plum lucky," Caleb said to Jamie. "Just like you said yesterday, we're scouts."

Tom corrected Caleb, "Not yet. Only couriers. We'll just be carrying messages."

"That's important enough," Caleb answered.

The advance began thirty minutes later, but it was 5 A.M. before the 23rd Virginia was in place. Colonel Titus V. Williams' Third Brigade, which included the 23rd, anchored its left flank south of the Chancellorsville Turnpike. A quarter mile to their front was General James Lane's Brigade and General Samuel McGowan's Brigade of A.P. Hill's Light Division. Lane's position was to the left and also anchored on the turnpike. McGowan's Brigade was on the right to the southeast.

General James Archer's Brigade was on McGowan's right. Facing these two brigades at Hazel Grove and extending north to the turnpike were the First and Third Division of Union General Daniel Sickles' Third Corps. Sickles' Second Division formed the extreme right flank of the Union line north of the turnpike, also known as the Plank Road.

Behind Sickles' Division was Union General William Hays'

Third Brigade of General William French's Third Division in Darius Couch's Second Corps. General Alpheus Williams' First Division, Slocum's Twelfth Corps, was positioned to support Sickles' center. The First and Third Brigades of Generals Knipe and Ruger were placed as strategic reserves. Colonel Samuel Ross' Second Brigade provided skirmishers in advance of the center and right of Sickles' line.

When Archer and McGowan advanced, they did not know that Union General Hooker had ordered Sickles to withdraw and join the main Union defenses. Only the Pennsylvanians of Charles Graham's Brigade and Huntington's artillery battery remained as Sickles' rear guard when the Confederate attack began. Archer's men swept the field of resistance and took more than 100 prisoners.

Archer, however, had lost track of McGowan. He was alone on the plateau of Hazel Grove. McGowan's regiments, for their part, had lost brigade-level cohesion in the dense pines and underbrush. In some cases, even companies within regiments became separated during the attack. In spite of these conditions, McGowan drove back the 37th New York.

McGowan's Brigade then stalled in a bloody thirty-minute firefight with Ruger after going only another 100 yards. Ruger's defense repelled McGowan's forces. The result was more confusion. McGowan was separated from Archer on his right and Lane on his left.

It was Lane's men who paid the price. Sending the untested Union 3rd Maryland to flight, Lane's brigade of mostly Tar Heels neutralized Union Colonel Dimick's gun section. Lane continued his advance, only to come under the well-aimed guns of additional Yankee artillery. In the attack, counterattack, and attack, Lane's four regiments lost eleven original and replacement commanders. Ruger's final attack, a charge with fixed bayonets supported by Mott's Brigade, drove Lane's Brigade back to the old Union position in complete panic and disarray.

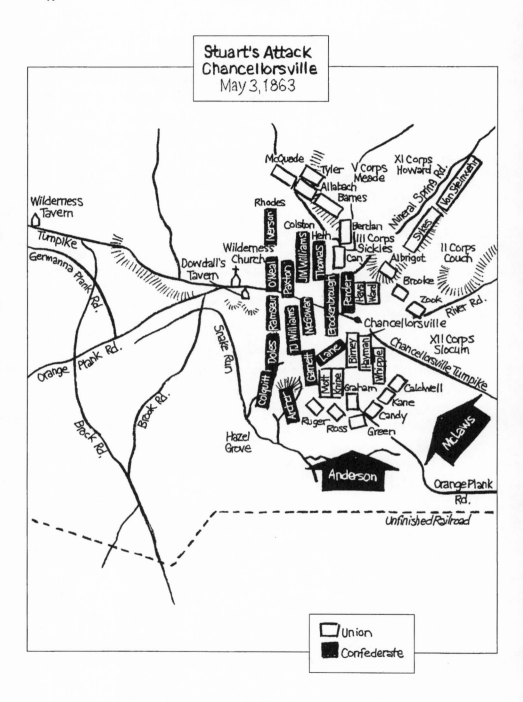

The brigades of Confederate Generals Edward Thomas and Dorsey Pender fared little better. Pender had launched an all-out assault at Union General Berry's fortifications. Brockenborough had come up in support of Thomas' and Pender's attack. Thomas directed his forces to sweep left and turn against Berry's apparently exposed right flank. The fire on both sides was murderous.

During an attempt by Berry to communicate directly with General Mott, a Confederate sharpshooter killed Berry. General Joseph Carr replaced Berry, as Thomas was succeeding in routing the Union right flank. The Union position now was desperate. Their fortunes reversed with the appearance of two brigades of Union General William French's Division on Thomas' left flank. Thomas' men fell back, then retreated, and finally fled. Pender had no choice but to withdraw as well to avoid a similar catastrophe.

Now, Stuart ordered his second line forward. Tom and Caleb were busy running orders to Colonel Walton of 23rd Virginia from Colonel Williams at Third Brigade Headquarters. Colston's Division was attacking over the decimated lines of Pender and McGowan, who remained under heavy fire. Reaching the line, Williams Third Brigade refused to advance any farther.

Tom watched Captain Tompkins frantically trying to move his men out from behind the works. They would not budge. Artillery shells exploded all around them. Minié balls whizzed by or popped as men were struck. Caleb later said that throughout the seesaw along the road, Simeon Walton refused to panic. Over and over he rallied his officers and men against their firmest resolve not to go forward to a certain death.

Casualties among the officers were as great as among the enlisted men. Titus Williams was wounded and replaced by John McDowell, who also was wounded. His replacement, Sam Walker, was killed. His replacement, Stephen Thruston, was wounded before command finally settled on Lieutenant Colonel Hamilton Brown. These changes occurred in the space of but two hours on that Sunday morning.

Then Paxton arrived with the Stonewall Brigade. Thomas Garnett with the Second Brigade soon followed him. The push was on, but again the effects of the terrain and the advantages of defense worked in the Yankees' favor.

Stuck in the bottomland with his regiments splintering farther and farther apart, Paxton tried to run between the gap in his line. A single shot put him on the ground. Lying on his back, he raised his right hand and placed it over his left breast pocket. Paxton's last act was to touch a photograph of his wife and his personal Bible.

Garnett suffered a similar fate. His brigade, like those of Pender, McGowan, Titus Williams, and Paxton, was smashed and sent reeling back to take cover among the bodies of the dead. Mortally wounded himself, Garnett was removed from the field and taken behind the lines.

The slaughter was crushing on both sides throughout the morning. Rebel and Yankee alike hoped for a quick death. Hatred covered the field like gunfire. No quarter was offered or given in the blackness of the battle. Mercy was shown only to comrades.

As he was bringing a message to Colston, Caleb looked across the battlefield. Two soldiers, one a Yankee and the other a Confederate, approached the Confederate position. The Yankee, dazed but still walking, was trying to hold in his intestines. The Confederate crawled, with his intestines dragging behind him. A clean shot put the Confederate out of his misery, but the Yankee was shot only in the leg to keep him from advancing.

As Caleb remounted, a round of solid shot tore through the left shoulder of a soldier only a few feet away. The man fell on his right side, exposing his still beating heart. Caleb sat still, shocked, as the heart slowed, then stopped. The man's grimy face and hollow mouth showed no sign of pain or agony, only the vacant look that is death.

Funk now commanded the Stonewall Brigade, which seemed to make up the whole of Colston's Division. With the division locked in place, Tom and Caleb settled in with what they could find left of the shattered and scattered 23rd Virginia. Yankee dead were stacked like cordwood and used for breastworks. One man had been disemboweled. Tom used his exposed hipbones as a prop to steady his aim.

Three events brought the morning's action to a close. Archer finally secured the high ground at Hazel Grove. This provided the opportunity for Confederate Colonel Porter Alexander to bring up the artillery and pound Ruger's Yankees with punishing fire. On the Confederate left, Iverson's Brigade dislodged Union General Williams and drove his forces into retreat back toward the main Union lines.

It was the third line attack by Rhodes Division, and specifically the brigades led by Doles and Ramseur, that ended Federal resistance. After defeating the attacks by Hill and Colston, and suffering from the artillery fire from Alexander's guns, Rhodes' assault became irresistible.

Doles and Ramseur had help, however. The Stonewall Brigade was fought out. When neither their commander, Paxton, nor Rhodes was able to motivate them to advance, Jeb Stuart appeared.

Stuart had been all over the battlefield encouraging one regiment or brigade after another. He waved his plumed hat and sang "Ole Joe Hooker" to the tune of the "Old Gray Mare." With Stuart's encouragement, the Stonewall Brigade joined the final thrust.

Coming out from behind the logworks abandoned by the Yankees they yelled, "Remember Jackson." Fear and exhaustion

were overcome by pride and competition with the North Carolinians. Ramseur remained contemptuous of the Virginians' behavior at Chancellorsville long after the battle, but the Stonewall Brigade gave them the edge to succeed.

Captain Bonham of the 3rd Alabama began the attack under orders directly from Rhodes. Bonham led his men out of
their position entirely alone and unsupported. Officers called
out to Bonham that he was crazy. He ignored their taunts.

Pride again overcame fear, as the regiments on either side of
Bonham followed him up the slope to Fairview. Fifty Union
cannon fired canister, shot, and grape, depending on what they
had left. Without adequate infantry support, however, the Union
line finally collapsed.

After four hours of fighting and at a terrible cost in life and
leadership, Stuart forced the Union army out of its new defenses. Hooker's army now was away from the heights at Fairview
and north of the Orange Plank Road. Lee brought the remainder of his forces up to join Stuart's right flank with his own left.

With artillery support from Alexander, Archer supported
Lee's forces as they forced Union generals Geary, Cross, Brooke,
and Meagher to remove their commands farther north. As this
initiative progressed, more cannon were brought to bear from
Fairview. Lee then turned his attention to the threat from
Sedgwick at Fredericksburg. For Tom and Caleb, the fight was
over.

In the midst of the chaos, no one noticed a shell fragment
strike the horse a young colored boy was sitting on. No one
noticed as the dazed boy started to stand up, only to be hit
himself by a bullet in his chest. As Jamie lay speechless, stunned,
bleeding, no one came to his aid.

Hours later, Caleb searched for Jamie. He found him where
he had fallen. Caleb wept as he buried him as deep as his fading
strength would allow. The hard red Virginia clay did not allow

much. Digging only four feet into the ground, Caleb piled rocks on the boy's body before replacing the earth. Jamie's death was a guilt that would follow him to his own dying day. It was well into the night before he rejoined Tom in camp. Chancellorsville changed many men, including Tom and Caleb, in ways they couldn't talk about.

When Hooker withdrew across the Rapidan, Lee took his army and returned to his previous positions at Fredericksburg. At Chancellorsville the 23rd Virginia reported ten killed, seventy wounded, and two missing. Tom, Caleb, and miraculously their horses had survived without a scratch.

Jackson did not recover from his wounds. His wife, Anna, and their five-month-old daughter, Julia, visited him. His spirits rose to see them, and it was thought that he would recover. It was Jackson's custom, however, to treat himself with cold towels laid across his abdomen. Unknown to his doctor, he requested that this be done by one of his aides. Within two days, pneumonia and other infections set in and he died.

After Jackson's death, Lee reorganized the Army of Northern Virginia into three corps. General Colston was relieved on May 28. Brigadier General George H. Steuart became the new commander in Major General Edward Johnson's Division of Ewell's Second Corps.

Colonel Walton formally mustered in Tom and Caleb as outriders for the 23rd Virginia. They each drew only two months wages as scouts, and the paperwork was never sent to Richmond or Raleigh, nor did their names appear on the muster rolls. Copies of their "enlistment" papers were among Walton's personal effects sent directly to the Parkers in North Carolina after the war.

The reorganization gave Caleb a chance to look for others like himself, and he found many. They were from Virginia, North Carolina, and Louisiana. A few were from Georgia. Most worked as ordinary farmers, but he found others, like himself, who were skilled in a trade.

Most had joined the army because it was "the right thing to do." Their homes and livelihoods were threatened. Of greatest importance, they saw themselves as different from slaves. They owed their community something and expected to better themselves by joining the fight.

Like Caleb, these free blacks slept and ate among their comrades, but not as true equals. They straddled the world between whites and slaves, without the privileges of one, but with more than the other. Fighting for the Confederacy proved their loyalty to their homes.

As part of the 23rd, Tom and Caleb stayed with the regiment on June 3 to guard the division trains, as Johnson's Division broke camp near Hamilton's Crossing. The move into Pennsylvania had begun. As part of the supply train entourage, Caleb and Tom did not participate in the engagement at Winchester on June 14 and 15.

On June 18 they crossed the Potomac at Boteler's Ford with the rest of Ewell's Corps. They continued through Maryland and into Pennsylvania where, at Greencastle, Steuart's entire brigade was ordered to McConnellsburg. They spent the next day collecting horses, cattle, and other supplies before rejoining Johnson's Division at Carlisle.

On the way to Carlisle, Tom pointed out how neat the farms were in Pennsylvania.

"Too bad we're gonna make a mess of them," Caleb replied.

"You mean like at Chancellorsville?"

"Or Perryville."

Tom shifted in his saddle. "Perryville was nothing like Chancellorsville."

"It's the belly wounds get me. A clean hit's all right. Kills a man or wounds him. Belly wounds are a slow death."

Tom was slow to answer. "Saw a man lose his jaw. Kept trying to push his tongue back in his mouth. If he lived, it won't be living."

"That, too," Caleb replied.

"And Jamie?"

Tears welled in Caleb's eyes, "Too hard, Tom."

"But was it quick?"

"Seems so. Got him clean in the chest. No way that child should of been there."

Tom felt Caleb's remorse. "We got drummer boys his age."

"They shouldn't be here either. This is men's fault and men's work."

"Ain't work," Tom responded. "Not like blacksmithing."

"Guess not. This is revenge. I can understand what gets into Tinker and Carter and the others."

"You mean revenge about my pa and yours?" Tom asked.

Caleb turned in the saddle. "That, too, but more."

"How so?"

"We had a good life," said Caleb. "This whole secession thing destroyed our lives. I didn't want nothing but to be left alone."

"That's sure enough, I reckon."

"For me, it ain't all though. Win or lose, I'm gonna lose. Won't be no right place for coloreds back home no how."

Tom was taken off guard. "So, what do you do after the war?"

"Probably can't live in the mountains no more. Don't know where I'd move to. Yankees don't treat coloreds much better than sothrens do. Least they could do is leave us alone. The other free nigrahs is feeling the same way."

"Guess you gotta think on it more," Tom said, knowing that Caleb was too caught up in thinking about after the war. Tom worried more about surviving it.

Carlisle had been a rich source of supply. Tom and Caleb ate well, as did their horses. The people were cold and dour in spite of Lee's orders to buy supplies, not steal them. Payment in Confederate script was, in the eyes of the Pennsylvanians, the same thing as theft.

Between June 19 and 29, Johnson's division countermarched to Greenville and then went east to Scotland. When they were ordered to Gettysburg, the supply train slowed their progress. Compounding the problem was the need to pass along Longstreet's column that was using the same road. As a result, they did not arrive in Gettysburg until after 6 P.M. on July 1.

Ewell's Corps arrived and formed on the left of Lee's army north of Benner's Hill. Johnson's Division was Ewell's left flank and Steuart's Brigade was Johnson's left flank. Only the 3rd North Carolina and 2nd Maryland Battalion were farther to the left than the 23rd Virginia.

Colonel Walton addressed the men of the 23rd after they had made camp. "The Yankees ran again," he declared confidently. "We attacked them and they ran. Howard's Dutchmen were cowards at Chancellorsville and they skedaddled again today. Tomorrow, we'll sweep them off that hill."

Even as Walton spoke, however, the men could hear the picks, axes, and shovels at work not 500 yards away. "We'll be attacking fortifications again," Tom said. "The sooner we get going, the better."

"Our instructions are to wait on General Longstreet's attack on the right," Walton continued. "Once Meade has drained his reserves to protect his left flank, it'll be our turn."

Caleb whispered to Tom, "Better hope Longstreet moves quick." Tom nodded his agreement.

8

CULP'S HILL

Morning came and went with no order to form up and advance. The same was true of the early afternoon. Walton's promises of the night before were hollow. At least that's what the men started to believe. Tom and Caleb knew better, but the delay made them more concerned. They had spent the day with Colonel Walton and General Steuart at General Johnson's Headquarters.

"They're gonna plan us to death," Caleb complained.

Tom nodded. "Those couriers are on Ewell's staff. I remember them from Chancellorsville."

As Tom spoke, they overheard General Johnson order General Jones to move a regiment south of Benner's Hill in support of Latimer's Battery that now occupied the hill. Latimer was reinforcing Dance's artillery that already was lobbing shells at Union General Wadworth's First Corps on the upper portion of Culp's Hill.

Jones sent Lieutenant Colonel Salyer's 50th Virginia. This regiment supplemented the four companies of the 25th Virginia that had been posted as skirmishers since the previous evening. In response to threatening action by Federal skirmishers directed at Latimer's battery, Jones also brought up the remaining companies of the 25th Virginia.

The skirmish line, placed under the command of Colonel John Higginbotham, became more aggressive in response to the Yankee incursions. Jones placed his remaining regiments, the 21st, 42nd, 44th, and 48th Virginia 300 yards behind the 50th Virginia and to the left of Latimer's artillery line.

With Jones' Brigade in place, Nicholls' and Steuart's brigades were instructed to cross Rock Creek and move into their assigned positions. The Stonewall Brigade, commanded by Colonel James Walker, was attempting to repulse Union cavalry on Brinkerhoff's Ridge. They were to join the other three brigades "as soon as possible." In the absence of the Stonewall Brigade, Johnson planned to bring 4,000 men against the Union position on Culp's Hill.

Tom and Caleb rode with Colonel Walton and his staff when the meeting with General Johnson was over. The ground over which the three brigades would pass was wooded and marshy around Rock Creek. Their front would angle southeast and stretch nearly 2,700 feet between the fence line at Benner's Hill and the woods on the slope at Wolf Hill.

Jones' Brigade went forward at 6:30 and immediately encountered stiff resistance from the Yankee skirmishers. After pushing the skirmishers back, Jones' men quickly crossed Rock Creek. Reforming into lines of stacked regiments that were each two-men deep, Jones ordered the advance at the base of the slope to Culp's Hill.

Nicholls' Brigade did not begin its advance until seven. Like Jones, Nicholls' had stacked his regiments to obtain a greater concentration in strength at the point of attack. Unlike Jones, the lead regiments of Nicholls' Brigade encountered no resistance from Yankee skirmishers.

In deploying into battle formation, the order of regiments

for Steuart's Brigade was reversed. Instead of being on the extreme left, the 3rd North Carolina formed Steuart's right and was to align itself on Nicholls' left. Steuart's advance, which began after that of Nicholls, was complicated by the need to wheel right. The 3rd North Carolina, with the shortest distance to achieve, succeeded.

The farther one of Steuart's regiments was from Nicholls' flank, the more difficult the terrain. These conditions considerably slowed the progress of the remainder of the brigade with predictable results. Gaps in the line occurred between the 3rd North Carolina and the 2nd Maryland and between the 2nd Maryland and the 23rd Virginia. Steuart's left wing then became separated from the left flank of the 23rd Virginia.

Colonel Walton was unhappy because the 23rd Virginia was not at its full strength. He did not know the location of four companies that were on detail as skirmishers. Two additional companies had been assigned to the 'brigade guard."

"You and Caleb can fight with the Richmond Sharpshooters," he said to Tom when they reached Rock Creek.

They dismounted and strung a rope between two trees. Tom and Caleb tethered their horses, drew ammunition from their saddlebags, and ran forward to join Captain Tompkins and the rest of the company.

"I wish Stonewall was here," a private named Ben Roberts said. "He always got the Yankees running while saving our hides."

"So I've heard," Tom interjected, "but Stonewall's gone. We gotta do with what we got."

"And that's the sad truth," Ben replied.

Captain Tompkins walked by, urging the men to be alert. Throughout the day skirmishers on both sides had been heavily engaged. Tompkins did not know, nor did anyone in Johnson's command, the strength of the Yankees or their entrenchments. He also did not know that Union General Geary had withdrawn Candy's and Kane's brigades an hour earlier.

As a result of Geary's actions, the 1,350-man brigade commanded by Brigadier General George Greene would take the brunt of Johnson's attack. Elements of Wadsworth's First Corps and Howard's Eleventh Corps were available as reinforcements. While Jones advanced his brigade toward the upper level of Culp's Hill, Greene was extending his line to cover his right flank.

The last of Geary's regiments, the 28th Pennsylvania, had left barely ten minutes before Jones' Brigade arrived. Greene first became aware of the attack when he heard the bugle call for assistance from his skirmish line. Lieutenant Colonel John Redington commanded the skirmish line that included fewer than 180 officers and men.

Greene ordered Lieutenant Colonel Herbert von Hammerstein's 200-man 78th New York down the slope to Rock Creek in support of Redington. Against Jones' entire brigade, this was an insufficient number of men. He also sent requests for reinforcements to Wadsworth on Cemetery Hill and Howard, whose forces were bivouacked to his rear.

Tom and Caleb heard the pop of musketry off to their right. The swell of battle increased. In front of them was not even a hint of resistance. They climbed through swales and pulled their brogans out of sticky soil. Colonel Walton and Captain Tompkins heard the gunfire too. The captain ordered the troops to wheel right again.

The men obeyed and slogged their way through the woods. Their lines were ragged and all semblance of order was lost. Moving up the slope, Tom and Caleb were slightly ahead of the forward line. The intensifying fire on their right made them more cautious. Staring intently into the growing darkness, they searched for any sign of movement. None was seen.

A courier arrived from the 2nd Maryland Battalion. They

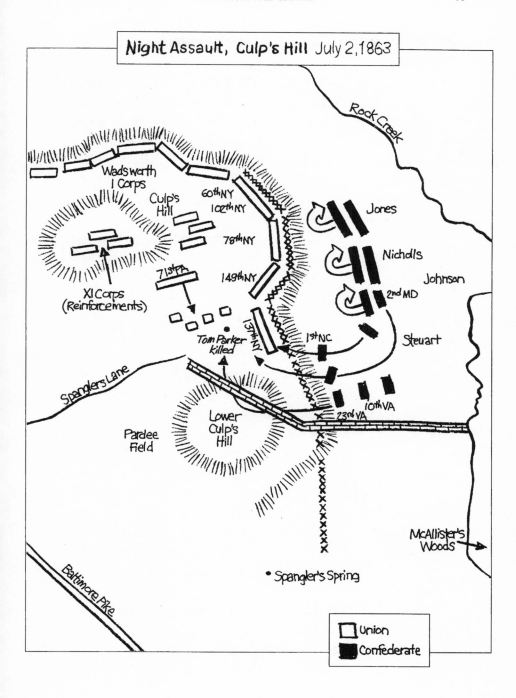

Night Assault, Culp's Hill July 2, 1863

were 100 yards ahead, to the right, and had found the left flank of the 3rd North Carolina. Steuart ordered Walton to move rapidly in support of his old regiment. The 23rd Virginia responded as quickly as the slope and dense trees would allow.

Suddenly, the woods in front of them exploded with the flash of rifle fire. The flames seemed to be launched forward at least five feet. Screams from the men of the 2nd Maryland followed. Their angry return volley followed their screams. At the top of the slope, there was no evidence that the volley had even a nominal effect.

What Tom and Caleb saw was the first volley from the 137th New York aimed in a northeast direction. They had fired not at the 1st Maryland, but at the 3rd North Carolina. Both regiments had returned fire. The 137th New York was the right leg of an entrenchment shaped like a V with the 149th New York occupying the left leg.

Being dug in near the top of Culp's Hill, the New Yorkers were protected by both elevation and their breastworks from return fire by the Confederates. Their position also reduced the effectiveness of their defensive fire. Most shots passed over the heads of Jones' and Nicholls' men. It was a stalemate, made worse by the steepness and rockiness of the slope these two Confederate brigades were trying to ascend.

Steuart realized that his left wing, beginning with the 23rd Virginia was beyond the Federal lines. In the fog of battle, the 137th New York was unaware of their presence. Steuart turned to Walton, who walked off, passing from company commander to company commander. Walton ordered them to hold fire and move to the left.

The 23rd Virginia only had to slip quietly over the breastworks to fire into the rear of the defending Yankees. Now moving steadily and as quietly as conditions would allow, Tom, Caleb, and their comrades resumed the climb. It was about

9:15 P.M. Unchallenged, fifty men climbed over the works vacated by McDougall's Union Brigade.

They turned and came into line below the summit of the lower level of Culp's Hill. Walton sent Lieutenant Charles Raines to confirm that the troops in front of them were the enemy. Raines reported that the New Yorkers were spaced more than a foot apart. Thus, the effectiveness of their fire was reduced. It was effective enough, however, given the protection offered by the pits they had dug and the breastworks in front of them. These pits now were a trap.

Before attacking, Walton needed to confirm that the 2nd Maryland could exploit the advantage that the 23rd could create. He went around to the right of his regiment and found Major Goldsborough, who was prepared to charge when Walton attacked.

When Walton sent Raines to confirm that it was the enemy to his front, he disclosed the Confederate presence on the Union right. In response, Colonel David Ireland, who commanded the 137th New York, turned Company A to meet the threat. The trap in the entrenchments now had lesser, but not insignificant, value.

Unknown to Walton, Steuart had sent Lieutenant Randolph McKim to bring the 1st North Carolina in support of the 3rd North Carolina. McKim, however, had made a terrible mistake. He positioned the 1st North Carolina to fire at what he believed were Union troops. In truth, they fired on the right wing of the 2nd Maryland and two companies of the 3rd North Carolina. His error helped stall the attack and added to the confusion.

"Fire!" Walton shouted. Nearly one-fourth of the men of Company A of the 137th New York fell dead or wounded. Only some of their number returned fire. Instead, they began edging their way down the trench to crowd the men next to them. The men of the 23rd reloaded as the New Yorkers scrambled to reorganize, and the 10th and 37th Virginia came into line on the 23rd's left.

Again the 23rd Virginia fired. The result was panic in the Union lines. Colonel Walton now expected the Yankee line to begin to roll up. He believed that this would relieve the pressure on the 2nd Maryland Battalion and allow them to charge as he had persuaded Goldsborough to do.

Goldsborough and his regiment's commander, Lieutenant Colonel James Herbert, however, were dealing with the panic on their right caused by the 1st North Carolina. He hesitated to order the charge because he believed that the Yankees somehow had slipped around behind him. Thus, the 23rd was momentarily the sole point of attack on the right flank of the 137th New York.

Believing that he would be supported by the 2nd Maryland, Walton ordered the 23rd across a small wall and toward the vacated Union position. There was a delay, but three companies of the 2nd Maryland suddenly appeared and the Union right collapsed. Goldsborough had resolved his "issue" with the 1st North Carolina. The 23rd Virginia rushed forward in support of Goldsborough's charge.

Tom was on Caleb's right and ten paces ahead of him when Tom stepped into the soft circle of light from the embers of a dying fire. Caleb saw the flash of the muskets and heard the bullets *p-z-z-z-t* as they flew by. Glancing in Tom's direction, Caleb saw one bullet strike Tom's left forearm shattering the bone. He also saw a second bullet hit Tom in the chest and pass through his body. Tom dropped to his knees still conscious but stunned. Another rifle fired from the darkness, Tom's head jerked back and to the left. He fell forward on his face with his body covering the small campfire.

The Confederate line exploded in counter fire, with Caleb

firing as fast as he could find a target. Caleb heard the men on the other side of the line screaming *"Gott in Himmel!"* He knew immediately that these were the men of Howard's Eleventh Corps. Both sides charged. Caleb ran to where Tom had fallen.

As he reached Tom's body, a Union soldier came at him with his bayonet pointed directly at his chest. Caleb fired his carbine from the hip. The soldier's rifle dipped forward driving the bayonet into the ground and propelling his body to Caleb's left.

Caleb rolled Tom's body off the fire and brushed away the embers. He looked into Tom's face. The third bullet had torn away Tom's lower right jaw and lodged in his brain. He was dead before his body hit the ground.

Looking up, Caleb saw two more soldiers rushing toward him. He was quick enough to dispatch one with a single shot from his carbine that struck the man in the face. His aim was deliberate. The second he had to deflect by using the carbine's barrel to drive the bayonet to his right. Nonetheless, the blade cut through his coat and made a gash on his right bicep.

Rising up from his knee, Caleb brought the stock of the carbine around to hit the soldier in the lower back. He could hear the man's bones break. When the man was on the ground, Caleb drew his knife, drove his knee between the man's shoulder blades, grabbed his hair, reached around, and slit his throat. There was a garbled cry that ended as the man's vocal chords were severed. The soldier's body relaxed, and Caleb pushed the man's face down in the mass of blood that flooded the ground.

Caleb stood up to see that the regiment had moved on in the direction of Spangler Lane. He returned to where Tom's body lay. "I won't let you rot here in Pennsylvania," he said softly. "You going home, Tom. You going home."

Caleb slung the two carbines over his left shoulder. Using both hands, he pulled Tom into a sitting position. Then, Caleb yanked hard on Tom's coat as he stood up. With a single smooth motion, Tom's body came to rest on Caleb's shoulder.

He had gone less than a dozen paces when a Union soldier dashed out of the trench to his left and charged straight at him. Caleb dropped Tom's body. The man was coming at him so fast that he couldn't swing his carbine around in defense. Instead, Caleb dropped to one knee and pulled out his boot knife. The Yankee kicked it away, but being balanced on one leg, Caleb threw him to the ground.

Before the Yankee could get back to his feet, Caleb kicked him in the face. His heavy boots knocked the man senseless. Caleb calmly picked up a large rock from the campfire. He smashed the rock repeatedly against the man's skull long after the man had died. His emotions spent, Caleb stood up, walked back to where Tom's body waited, and picked him up once more.

To make good his withdrawal, Caleb had two obstacles to overcome. The first was carrying Tom along the slope that was the saddle nearest the lower level crest of Culp's Hill. Compared to maneuvering his way over the Union entrenchments and breastworks that followed, the slope was easy. Twice he tried and failed. He finally decided to carry Tom farther east until the trenches ended. Still he could not get the body over the tangle of logs. In frustration, he dismantled a section of the works so that he could push the body through the opening. He was exhausted. Caleb sat down on the slope once he was satisfied that Tom was outside the Yankee lines.

The sounds, sights, and smell of the battle were still evident. He could see the flash of the rifles 200 hundred yards to the west. "Must be the rest of the 2nd Maryland," he thought to himself. Then he thought, no, they must have crossed over into the Yankee lines. Perhaps those were North Carolina boys over there.

More rifle fire followed. He heard the Rebel yell and saw

men moving quickly toward the Yankee lines. "Go get 'em," he said loudly and hoarsely. "Kill them Yankee bastards!" A flash of return fire, however, took the steam out of the Carolinians charge. They still were at least fifty yards from the federal lines; certainly they were no closer.

Behind him, somewhere that seemed very far away, he heard the Rebel yell again. He heard screams, shouts, and the sound of men in hand-to-hand combat. For a very small moment Caleb thought about returning. Tom, he decided, was his priority. The struggle on the other side of the breastworks suddenly was punctuated with volley after volley of rifle fire. Caleb counted the seconds and the minutes between the volleys.

He felt strong enough to continue and hoisted Tom across his right shoulder once again. It was 300 yards to Rock Creek and another twenty-five to where the horses were tethered. His return was made easier because it was downhill. The rocks and trees still provided formidable obstacles. He stopped to rest three times before reaching Rock Creek.

At that point the soft ground slowed him. He then had to cross the creek and avoid slipping on the rocks and pebbles. He collapsed when he reached the other side. Caleb called out for the horses, hoping they would whinny or snort so that he could determine their location. He heard nothing, so he headed to where he thought they might be.

His sense of direction was off in the dark, but not too far off. He ended up ten yards behind them. Caleb staggered forward and slid Tom's body to the ground. He guessed that it must be sometime between 11 P.M. and midnight. It had taken more than an hour to carry Tom some 450 yards over the difficult terrain.

Caleb could still hear gunfire. Heavy gunfire. Johnson's assault was about to end for the night. In the partially moonlit darkness, neither Federal nor Confederate knew exactly where their enemy might be waiting. There was a price to pay in learning the truth.

For the unfortunate Confederates, the night provided the Federals with the opportunity to bring back the remainder of Slocum's Twelfth Corps. The arriving Federals, however, repeatedly stumbled into Steuart's regiments that now occupied positions all over the lower level of Culp's Hill and the general vicinity of Spangler's Spring. Over the next several hours, more then 100 Yankees were killed or wounded and half again that many were captured.

Caleb remained with the horses. Tom's body was only a few feet away. He slept for not more than two hours. It was the sleep of physical exhaustion, fraught with nightmares. He could not escape the feeling that Tom's spirit sheltered and protected him. Finally, the restlessness of his distracted sleep brought him back to consciousness. He could sleep no more.

He took a long drink of the warm water in his canteen. With the same fluid motion, Caleb reached down, grabbed Tom's coat, and pulled the body over his shoulder. He placed Tom across his horse's saddle and tied his hands and feet to keep his body from sliding off. Mounting his own horse, Caleb began the trip around the eastern slope of Benner's Hill.

There still was the sound of occasional rifle fire. More dominant, however, was the creaking sound of wagon wheels on the Baltimore Pike. Caleb also heard the movement of a large number of men behind him just as he turned northwest on the other side of Benner's Hill. These men most likely belonged to Ruger's Brigade. They were returning to McAllister's Woods, southeast of where Steuart's Brigade had attacked the Union right flank.

The horses plodded on. Caleb slouched in the saddle. He rode another twenty or maybe thirty minutes and Caleb knew that the camp was near. "Who goes there? Gotcha covered!" said a voice from his left.

"Caleb Parker, 23rd Virginia," he answered, as he relaxed his grip on the reins and let the horses come to a stop.

The voice called out again, "Don't know no Caleb Parker. Stand down!"

Caleb dismounted. Six men came out of the woods along the trail. A different voice said, "That's the nigrah joined us back in Chancellorsville, fool. Give him a hand. He's got a wounded man with him."

"Not wounded," Caleb replied. "Dead."

"Where's the other boys?" someone who Caleb thought might be a private named Burch or Burke asked.

Caleb glanced around. "Back on that hill somewhere."

The same man asked another question, "Why you here?"

"I need to see Lieutenant DePriest," Caleb replied. "It's a mess up there."

Burch and another private took Caleb into camp. DePriest had not returned. First Lieutenant Christian Ludman was in charge in Captain Tompkins absence. "You a courier?" Ludman asked.

"Not official," said Caleb.

"What can you tell me?"

"The brigades of General Jones and Colonel Williams (Nicholls) are still in the woods. They're maybe seventy-five yards from the Yankee works. 2nd and 3rd North Carolina the same," Caleb began. "Pretty well pinned down, I reckon."

Ludman was expressionless. "What about Steuart and the 23rd?"

"We went over the works," Caleb answered. "2nd Maryland on our right. Not sure if it the 10th or 37th Virginia was on our left. No Yankees. Gone, plum empty."

"And then?"

"We charged, Lieutenant," said Caleb. "Charged and they ran."

Ludman sensed the weariness in the man. "What happened then?" he asked, probing for details.

"It gets hard now, sir." Caleb offered. "Tom got shot up real bad. It was Germans. Eleven Corps again. I shot two when they charged. Third one, I stabbed. The last, well, smashed his face with a rock."

Noticing the blood on Caleb's right arm and the torn cloth of his sleeve, Ludman believed him. "Where was the rest of the 23rd?"

"Up ahead somewhere. I couldn't tell. Decided then and there to bring Tom down the hill and back to camp."

"Why'd you do that?" Burch interjected.

Caleb was startled by the question. "Gotta take him home. Bury him with his kin. Ain't no other way. This is a lonely place for a mountain boy."

Ludman knew Caleb wasn't a coward. Caleb's intense stare unsettled him. No black man ever looked at a white the way Caleb looked at him now. He saw the sorrow in his eyes and took no offense. "I understand, Caleb. Can you tell me any more?"

"Yes, sir. There's Yankees coming up all over that hill. I heard them. Ain't no retreat. It's reinforcements. Steuart's in serious trouble."

9

SOUTHERN JOURNEY

S teuart moved his brigade back behind the Union works. Every incident during the night told him that he was about to be flanked or, worse still, enveloped. He conferred with Johnson then realigned his right flank with the left flank of the 1st North Carolina.

The 1st and 3rd North Carolina faced west, but the remainder of Steuart's regiments with the 2nd Maryland at the angle faced southwest. Nadenbousch's 2nd Virginia, facing south, protected Steuart's left flank. Behind the brigades of Steuart, Nicholls, and Jones now were the Stonewall Brigade plus those of O'Neal and Daniel.

Johnson's attack began at dawn. Yankee intentions to drive Johnson from the field opened at daybreak. Caleb already had left with Tom's body once again thrown over the back of his horse. He left before the remaining companies of the 23rd Virginia had joined their comrades on the battle line.

In the battle at Culp's Hill on July 2 and 3, the 23rd Virginia lost twenty-four men captured, two killed, and two wounded. Caleb heard the sounds of the early morning battle as he rode north of the town of Gettysburg. He was not tempted to return and join the attack. The thought sickened him. He would have no more of war. Its outcome no longer interested him. Grief and only grief filled him.

Caleb was searching for specific items, things he would need before his journey could begin. He easily located a saw, auger, hammer, and some bolts from an abandoned farm. His first priority, however, was sewing Tom's body into a tent half he found left on the battlefield.

The carnage of the first day north of Herr Ridge provided most of the remaining things he needed. He found five broken caissons within several hundred feet of one another. One suffered only from a broken tongue, which Caleb removed entirely. He then disassembled its ammunition case and replaced it with a flat platform.

He drilled holes in the axles near the wheel mounts and on the crossbeams for the platform. Using the bolts, he attached the longer tongues from two badly damaged wagons. His product was a rudely crafted, but strongly built, dogcart.

He then went to work on a makeshift casket. It was not as airtight as he would have liked, but it was sufficient for his needs. He lined it with tarred canvas and placed it on the cart. Once the casket was firmly in place, he laid Tom's canvas-encased body in it. Before putting the lid on, he placed the ammunition bags near Tom's head and the gunsmith's tools at his feet. The Parker carbines, sewn into the tarred canvas bags, were laid gently on either side of the body. He kept only his pistol and knife for protection.

Confederate infantry and cavalry passed by all day. None had expressed even a passing interest in his activities. Around midday, Caleb heard the beginning of the cannon bombardment that preceded what would become known as Pickett's Charge. The explosions spooked the horses. Fortunately, Caleb had secured them tightly to a damaged wagon. If he had not, they most certainly would have run off.

Caleb fashioned a harness for the dogcart. With only the casket for added weight, a single horse could pull it easily. He greased the wheels before saddling his horse, the final step. The job had taken him nearly the entire day.

It was after 5 P.M. when he started west on the Chambersburg Pike. He rode until darkness and weariness forced him to stop for sleep. He awoke to a cool and refreshing rain on the morning of July 4. Sitting up and gazing around, he struggled to remember where he was. The casket on the dogcart was an abrupt reminder. The horses were tethered only a few feet away.

Breakfast was crude compared to home, but sumptuous compared to army fare. He found wild raspberries and he had cheese that he had brought from the farmhouse when he foraged for tools. It was complimented by bread and hard cider.

Hitching his own horse to the dogcart, Caleb saddled Tom's horse as his mount. He turned south as soon as a decent road was available. He had no intention of going as far as Chambersburg. His only objective was to swing out away from the battlefield and the Confederate army.

When he set out on that morning, he was already through the gap and well south of Fairfield. He was grateful that he'd ridden through Fairfield at night. No one was around to ask questions. At his current pace, it would take more than a full day to reach Hagerstown.

The light rain turned to mist and then stopped. Half an hour later, the mist began again and turned to light rain. Again, the rain ended, but another cycle started an hour later. On impulse, he opened his haversack, removed his "free papers," and placed them in his shirt pocket. He buttoned the pocket flap and re-buttoned his vest.

The rain became heavier by afternoon. Mud slowed his pace. Caleb prayed the cart wouldn't become stuck in a rut. His prayers were answered, but he still was five miles from Hagerstown when he finally gave in for the night. He had decided to stop when a flash of lightening illuminated a dilapidated barn.

The route through the field was easier going than on the road. He found a section of the barn that leaked less than the rest and unhitched his horse. Using the saddle as a pillow, with two blankets under him on a pile of damp hay and one as a cover, he made a satisfactory bed.

He thought about what he might face as he drifted off to sleep. If Lee was defeated at Gettysburg, he would be retreating down this road. How soon? If Lee won, the road would be open until Caleb crossed into Virginia and onto the pike up the Shenandoah Valley.

The next morning was cool and dry, but the roads remained muddy. There was no sound of Lee and his army. Caleb rotated horses. He saddled his own and hitched Tom's horse to the cart. Returning to the road, he saw cavalry coming up behind him. The Confederate horsemen rode past him at a gallop. Caleb could tell by their faces that Lee had lost. He picked up the pace as much as he dared, reaching Hagerstown in late morning.

With the army headed his way, his goal was the fords at Williamsport or Falling Waters. He knew the Potomac was flooded and was expected to remain so for several days. He could make for these fords, but would have to wait for the floodwaters to subside. He could be trapped between Lee's army and the Potomac River.

Harper's Ferry was twenty miles due south. Trying to cross the Potomac at Harper's Ferry presented a greater risk—becoming trapped between the two armies. If he chose that route, Caleb would stay west of Antietam Creek and the Shenandoah Mountains for as long as possible.

He knew he had to choose soon. The van of the Confederate army, with wagonloads of supplies and the wounded, was already beginning to enter Hagerstown. If this was like Chancellorsville, the walking wounded would be looking for transportation. His cart could be confiscated and Tom's casket left by the side of the road.

Riding without Tom's protection or that of the Confederate army meant that he might be challenged as an escaped slave. His free papers could be confiscated or thrown away. Tom might never reach home for burial. This was the most serious risk of trying to cross at Harper's Ferry.

Caleb had always known that his freedom was fragile. It depended on the good will of a few whites. Any whites he might encounter now would be strangers. At home, the rules were known and the white Parkers sheltered the black Parkers. He decided that the known was better than the unknown and continued in the direction of Williamsport.

The Confederate army occupied Hagerstown on July 7 and began forming a line that arced from Conococheague Creek on its left and the Potomac River on its right. The Union army anchored its right on Antietam Creek near Hagerstown and its left in the Shenandoah Mountains one mile west of Rohrsville. In hindsight, Caleb thought that Harper's Ferry might have been a better choice.

For the next several days, Caleb kept himself hidden among the wagons. He spent his time with the slaves and freeman supporting the army. By staying behind the lines, Caleb was able to avoid contact with soldiers. On July 11, Lee began moving the wounded across the Potomac at both crossings. Caleb simply hitched Tom's horse to the cart and made his way into Virginia.

When Union General Kilpatrick's cavalry engaged Henry Heth at Falling Waters, Caleb, the wagons, and the advance guard were sixteen miles northeast of Winchester. The pace was slower than Caleb preferred, but the alternative of riding ahead of the van was less preferable. He needed to get as far up the Shenandoah Valley as possible before leaving the army entirely.

The lead columns held up for three more days below Winchester. Caleb was close to making his final decision about heading southeast. He had noticed that a number of the wounded soldiers were gathering on the western side of the camp. He decided to take a chance and talk with them.

"Where y'all from?" he'd ask a group. Most were from somewhere along the Blue Ridge. A few were from other parts of the South. Mountain men seemed to be converging away from the main body of the army. At the eighth or ninth such group, he asked, "Where y'all from?"

"Ashe County," came the reply as if the questioner would know that it was in North Carolina. "Where you from, boy?"

"Finally," Caleb said with a smile. "I'm from Waynesville. Name's Caleb Parker."

"Reckon you're looking for North Carolina boys."

Caleb nodded. "I'm taking a body home for burying."

"Your master?"

"No, sir, I was born free. Got my free papers with me," Caleb answered.

"This got something to do with us?" the soldier asked.

"Just want to ride with you," Caleb answered.

"Ride? All of us gotta walk," another soldier interjected. Pointing to the stump where his leg once was, he added, "I can't walk far or go fast on a crutch. Stump wants to bleed."

Caleb looked back at the soldier. "If you don't mind riding on a casket, you'll ride now. Get home faster, too."

"Can you handle two?" a third soldier asked.

"If we stay on the road, sure enough," Caleb replied. "In the mountains, it'll be tough."

The second soldier leaned forward. "Your friend a gunsmith?"

"Him and me both," Caleb answered.

"I hearda you and him, too," said the first soldier. "Never had the pleasure. Didn't rightly make the connection."

The third soldier frowned. "Heard you boys was Yankees."

"Lotsa folks thought that," Caleb said. "Tom wanted to fight in Tennessee. Rode with militia awhile. After the Yankees killed our fathers, Tom reckoned it was time to jine a real army. Hooked up with the 23rd Virginia."

"Jined and got killed himself," the second soldier said.

"Should be no doubt about his loyalties, now," Caleb said.

The first soldier asked, "How come you didn't stay and fight?"

"Seen enough," Caleb replied. "Here, Tennessee, and Kentucky."

"Without missing a leg, guess I have, too," said the first soldier. "Lotsa boys have. Mountains back home are full of 'em."

"I told you my name," Caleb said. "What are yours?"

"Wilson Wyatt," said the third soldier. "My brother Reed is coming, too."

"T. J. Carter," the first soldier said.

"Name's George Grimsely. We're all from Company A of the 26th North Carolina. Go by the Jeff Davis Mountaineers," the second soldier replied. "I was a prisoner at Fort Columbus til last August. Put me with the 61st. Decided I come back to the 26th."

"Reed's off scrounging food with Lee Ballou," Wilson offered. "It'll take us a week or more to get home. Hoping they get more laudanum. Don't have much left. Pain's awful."

T. J. said, "Ballou and me could hang around. Ain't wounded that bad. Our family's are in a bad way back home. Women folk just can't keep up the farms."

"Same here," Caleb added. "Just my little brother at the shop. Not much work like afore the war, but too much for him by his own self." No one said anything for a few awkward moments. "How'd 'yall lose your legs?" Caleb asked.

George looked at Wilson for a moment and then answered, "First day. Yankee artillery shell. Wilson and me was marching aside one another. Hit him above the knee and me below mine."

"So how'd you get this far?"

Reed Wyatt, who walked up behind Caleb, answered. "Cap'n McMillan said General Lee was planning on leaving a bunch a the wounded behind. George's brother and I wouldn't let him be in a Yankee prison. Our mamas would never let us hear the end of it."

"Lowry coming, too?" T.J. asked Reed, referring to George's brother.

Reed looked at T.J. sternly. "He'll catch up. Jesse Reeves is watching him closely. Jesse's a second lieutenant," he added for Caleb's benefit.

"Got us a ride for Wilson and George," T.J. said. "This here's Caleb Parker. Taking his friend home to bury him. He's got a cart for them to ride on."

"Won't ride with no traitor. I heard about them taking off. You know he's a free nigger," Reed said bitterly.

Caleb was silent. T.J. came to his defense, "Tom Parker was fighting with the 23rd Virginia when he died. So was Caleb."

Reed glared at Caleb, "Not what I heard. Didn't you take off with that bastard Bryson?"

"People thinks that," Caleb said, knowing he had to lie. "But I know better. When Tom and me came back from Tennessee, we heard Bryson was looking for us the night we left. We'd already got away."

"You better not be lying, boy. If you are, you're dead," Reed responded.

"Don't know how your brother got this far. I'll go on my way if y'all don't want my help," Caleb answered.

Reed stopped to think a minute before he spoke. "All right, I reckon. If he died fighting for the cause, you can ride with us."

"We was with Pettigrew on July 3," T. J. interjected. "Pickett's men were slaughtered and so were we. There were just sixty-seven of us reported for duty on July 4th. First day, we whupped them Yanks. Iron Brigade they was, too. Now we're running with our tails atween our legs. This was a useless fight. Fourteen boys from Company A are dead and the rest captured or wounded. For what?"

"Lotsa boys took French leave when they heard we was going into Pennsylvania. These were the smart ones. Damn Lincoln thinks we're fighting to keep our slaves," George added. "I didn't give up my leg over a damn nigger." George paused.

Caleb understood both the man's feelings and his discomfort. "I didn't lose my friend over slaves neither. Yankees won't leave us be. We had a good blacksmith and gunsmith business before the war. Three of us dead now. Me and my brother all's left."

Reed changed the subject. "We got some food but not much. Maybe a couple days. Ballou's looking for laudanum."

"We going up the valley pike?" Wilson asked.

"Past Danville, over the mountains, and onto Mount Airy," T. J. said. "Probably pass by Martinsville again."

Reed said, "There's a couple farms might help us out. We got kin afore we go into the Blue Ridge. Lee was talking to a sutler. Hope he can buy us a few things."

"He had twenty dollars," Wilson said. "Even so, might not buy much. If he's looking for laudanum, sutlers don't have much left except corn likker."

Caleb excused himself to go get the cart and his horses. He returned to find the North Carolinians bedded down. The man who must have been Lee Ballou was back since there were five men now. Caleb wasn't sure he trusted Reed Wyatt. There were more men like him than men like T. J. Carter. Reed reminded him entirely too much of Tinker Dave. Still, he decided, this was the safest way home.

Caleb woke earlier than the others. Lee Ballou was the only one up and about. "The rest of the army won't reach here for another eight to ten days," Lee said. "We'll be almost home by then."

"Hope so," Caleb replied as he began hitching his horse to the cart.

"Boys say there's a body in that box. That so?" Lee asked.

"Tom Parker was my best friend. Never once treated me wrong," Caleb answered. Caleb noticed that Ballou was struggling with his gear. "Need help?"

Ballou looked up and smiled. "Reckon. If you will."

Caleb knelt down and wordlessly rolled the man's blanket. Then, he tied the leather thong securely. "Left arm?" he asked.

"Twice," Ballou replied. "No broken bones. Tore up some muscle, though. It'll be months before I can hold a rifle. Thanks for the help."

"How'd you get Wilson and George this far?" Caleb asked.

"Wasn't easy. Captain McMillan let us carry them on litters. Men in the company who could took turns," Lee answered. Almost lost them when we turned to fight at Hagerstown. When the Yankee cavalry attacked at Falling Waters, thought we'd have to leave them there."

Caleb was puzzled. "Since you're this far, why not let the army take them to Richmond?"

"Family can care for them better. Too many men die or disappear," Lee said. "It's a risk. Wilson's stump bleeds sometimes. Better with us than with the army."

Caleb understood. He'd seen the hospitals. Worse still, he'd seen men with gangrene. The rest of the men were up now except for Wilson. Reed said to Lee, "Hope Wilson makes it. He lost a lot a blood and he's weak."

"Swears he can feel the leg," Ballou said in reply, as if to agree with the seriousness of Reed's brother's condition. "Phantom's got him."

"They can lay down between the wheels and the casket. More than enough room," Reed said. T. J. helped Reed put Wilson on the right and then George on the left.

"That body's more than a week old. How come it don't stink?" George asked.

"Wrapped it double. Used tarred cloth, too. Wouldn't advise you opening it up though."

George chuckled. "Reckon I wouldn't."

Wilson slept for most of the next three days. He barely spoke. George Grimsley joked and talked and dozed only on occasion. They stopped at a farmhouse to change Wilson's bandages. A black line running into his groin was plain to see. He had gangrene.

They knew it wouldn't be long and decided to stay there until he died.

"Want to take him home?" Caleb asked Reed once he was gone.

Reed looked surprised. "Would," he said.

Caleb built another casket, wrapped the body, and nailed the top on tight. He could see that Reed's attitude toward him was slowly changing.

Lowry Grimsley caught up with them before they left. He arrived on horseback. No one asked the source of his mount. George rode the rest of the way atop the two caskets.

The climb into the Blue Ridge was arduous, and the horses labored. Caleb changed the harness to accommodate both of them. Three spokes on the left wheel broke when the cart crossed a deep rut covered by fallen brush.

Lowry Grimsley rode to the next village. He returned an hour later with a wagon and two replacement wheels. Caleb, Lowry, and Reed repaired the cart. The entire group was in the village forty-five minutes later enjoying North Carolina hospitality. Two days later, they arrived in Jefferson. Caleb was given enough food to finish his journey home.

Reed Wyatt and his family were the most generous. "I've never trusted free nigras," he said. "Always thought they'd turn the slaves against us. You and that dead boy not jining in the beginning made me more suspicious."

"How'd you know about us?" Caleb asked.

"Y'all made the best guns in the mountains," he replied. "Folks know you. They know all about you. Took a few weeks, but the story got here."

Caleb was surprised. Reed shook his head. "What I know is you treated me and mine right. That means a little bit." He turned and walked away. It was the closest he could come to thanking Caleb.

Caleb snapped the reins and drove the cart out of Jefferson. It took two more days to reach Asheville. The valley was as beautiful as he remembered.

What he found to be less beautiful was the number of slaves. White families from Charleston and New Orleans had fled those cities. Many were leading members of southern society. Confederate General Leonidas Polk had moved his wife and twenty slave families to Asheville. His daughter, Katherine, followed after her house in Mississippi was destroyed. Senator Semmes of New Orleans had sent his family and house slaves to Hendersonville.

When Caleb left the mountains, there were very few slaves. Now, their population seemed larger than that of the whites. The slave auction was the most disappointing sight. Slave trading before the war was between the buyer and seller. It was a private affair. What Caleb saw was more like what he'd seen in Charleston. The auction was still a cruel affair only on a smaller scale. Men and women stripped to be prodded and poked by their potential buyers.

Thoughts of Jamie came to mind, filling his eyes with tears. He drove the memory away. Exhaustion was his excuse for feeling so sad when he should be glad about returning home. "Wish Tom was riding home with me," he said out loud.

Caleb was glad to put Asheville behind him. The town had changed. The war and Yankee invasions had changed it. He pushed the horses on. There was a spot along the road to Waynesville he wanted to reach before nightfall. Finding the grove, he guided the horses off the road.

Caleb placed the blade of his knife into the seam of the casket's lid and gently pried the top off. Maggots covered the tarred canvas. The smell sickened him. He resisted the urge to heave, but it was a futile attempt. When he was able, Caleb climbed back on the cart and removed the tarred canvasses with the carbines.

Taking his knife, he ripped open the stitches at the stock end of each bag. He slid the carbines out and wiped away the few maggots. His own carbine was placed in its saddle holster. Tom's carbine was propped up against a wheel.

Caleb pulled out the haversacks with the ammunition and gunsmith's tools. The bags were imbued with the stink of death. Otherwise, the contents were safe. Replacing the lid on the makeshift casket, Caleb returned to the road for the six-mile ride to Waynesville. He waited until morning to finish the last mile home. It had been nearly a month since he left Gettysburg.

10

ARRIVAL AND RENEWAL

Susan Parker had just finished milking the two remaining cows. Caleb saw her from a distance walking back from the barn before she heard the sound of the cart. He pulled back on the reins. The horses stopped. Susan looked up and saw him with a carbine resting across his lap, the cart, and its cargo.

Caleb had tried to prepare himself for this. He had dreaded telling Tom's mother what happened more than anything else he could imagine. Caleb and Susan now faced each other silently, her eyes barely visible in the shade from a tree.

Susan abruptly realized she was standing where she stood when the Yankees had hanged John from that same tree. Caleb urged the horse forward and the wheels of the cart creaked. Susan stared at the box on the cart, unmoving.

George came out of the foundry, wiping his forehead. Caleb motioned to him not to say anything. His eyes still focused on Susan, who had started walking slowly toward him. When finally he could see her eyes, he saw no tears, only the blank look of shock.

When she opened her mouth, Caleb was surprised. It was not so much a scream as a wail, a long piercing howl. Her cry brought the others running. They stopped as soon as they saw Caleb and the cart.

Caleb climbed off the cart. Susan reached for him, trapping Tom's carbine between them. She began to sob. George and the others approached. Their tears made it plain that all of them understood. Susan slowly regained her composure.

"George," Caleb said, "we need to dig a grave. Go get the shovels." George nodded and walked toward the toolshed. Caleb faced his family. "When George and me are done, I'll come get you."

"What happened?" Annie asked.

"Later. I want to get him buried. He's been dead a long time," Caleb answered.

George returned with two shovels. They removed the casket from the cart and took it to the family graveyard 200 yards downhill from the house. It was an hour before they returned to the house.

The usually active Susan sat in shock like a stone statue, her Bible in her lap. This was not the reaction Caleb expected or feared. Annie and Maggy sat on the floor resting their heads against her. Melinda was taking bread from the oven and humming softly, sadly.

The girls moved away, leaving Caleb and Susan alone.

"Did he die fast?" Susan asked. Caleb nodded. "Were you there?"

"Very close by. Bullets whizzed by me. Strange I wasn't killed, too," he answered.

They left the house and walked slowly to the burial ground, Susan leaning on Caleb for support. Her eyes were wet with tears. "I'm glad you got home safe, Caleb. Both of you are dear to me."

They walked on in silence. After reaching the open grave, Susan's hands worked through her Bible to find the verses that

she'd chosen. In Second Samuel she found David's lament for
Abner:

> *Thine hands were not bound*
> *Thine feet were not fettered*
> *You fell as one falls before wicked men.*

She modified David's curse on Joab and read with bitter-
ness, "May his blood fall upon the Yankees and all of their house-
holds." Again, she searched for the words to express her anger
and grief, reading from Daniel:

> *With a large army he will stir up his strength against*
> *the king of the South. The king of the South will wage*
> *war with a large and powerful army, but he will not*
> *be able to stand because of the plots devised against*
> *him. Those who take from the king's provisions will try*
> *to destroy him; his army will be swept away, and many*
> *will fall in battle.*
>
> *The two kings, their hearts bent on evil will sit at the*
> *same table and lie to each other, but to no avail, be-*
> *cause an end will still come at its appointed time. The*
> *king of the North will return to his own country with*
> *great wealth, but his heart will be set against the holy*
> *covenant.*
>
> *He will take action against it and then will return to*
> *his own country . . . At the appointed time he will*
> *invade the South again, but this time the outcome will*
> *be different from what it was before.*

The words took the fury from her. Sissy's arms went around
her and she wept. George stood behind his mother with the
others. Caleb was alone on the other side of the grave. "The
Lord is my Shepherd," he began. Melinda joined him, then
George, and Tom's sisters.

Susan pulled back from the comfort of Sissy's arms and stood up straight. One last time she searched her Bible for the words she needed. It was a familiar passage from Romans that soothed her soul and dulled her grief.

> *On your account we are being killed all day long; we are considered sheep for slaughter. But in all these things we are more than conquerors through Him who loved us. For I am convinced that neither death nor life, nor angels nor authorities, neither present nor future affairs, neither powers of the heights nor of the depths, nor anything else created will be able to separate us from the love of God that is in Christ Jesus our Lord.*

When she finished, they repeated the Lord's Prayer together. In the silence that followed, Caleb said, "There's a song Tom liked. He particularly liked these last two verses." His voice rang out,

> *Go forth in the pathway our forefathers trod;*
> *We too fight for freedom, our Captain is God,*
> *Their blood in our veins with the honors we vie;*
> *Their's too was the watchword, "We conquer or die."*
> *Their's too was the watchword, "We conquer or die."*
>
> *We strike for the South: Mountain, Valley and Plain,*
> *For the South we will conquer, again and again,*
> *Her day of salvation and triumph is nigh,*
> *Our's then be the watchword, "We conquer or die."*
> *Our's then be the watchword, "We conquer or die."*

As Caleb and George began to shovel dirt over the casket, Sissy began one last hymn and the others joined in.

> *Softly now the light of day*
> *Fades upon our sight away;*
> *Free from care and labor free,*
> *Lord, we would commune with Thee.*
> *Thou, whose all pervading eye*

Naught escapes, without, within,
Pardon each infirmity,
Open fault, and secret sin.
Soon from us the light of day
Shall forever pass away;
Then, from sin and sorrow free,
Take us, Lord, to dwell with Thee. Amen.

After Tom was laid to rest, Caleb fashioned a wooden headstone braced with an iron band. Alone he set it in place and for the first time cried deeply. It was his last farewell to Tom.

In the days, weeks, and months that followed, Caleb and George worked at blacksmithing. The strangeness and loneliness of not having his father, John, or Tom in the shop often overcame Caleb. In spite of George being his brother, working with him was like working with a stranger

Nonetheless, the brothers made a living for their family. Susan and Sissy relied on them. They all continued to work the small farm for food, but the extras came from the blacksmith's shop. As before, Confederate script was spent immediately; payment in silver or gold coin was saved.

In mid-December 1863, Caleb heard a rider approach and looked out the door to see a man in his mid-forties, well dressed in a coat with a black lamb's wool collar. His horse was a large dapple-gray stallion. The man dismounted and walked to the entrance where Caleb stood.

"Are you Caleb Parker?" he asked.

"I am," Caleb answered.

The man glanced around, "The gun maker?"

"Yes," said Caleb hesitantly.

Again the man glanced around. He seemed to be looking for something. "You the only ones here?"

"Yes," Caleb said again with the same hesitancy. "I don't

know your name, sir," he added without trying to sound too curious.

"I was expecting a white man, not two darkies," he said, ignoring Caleb's implied question.

"John and Tom were killed by Yankees. My Pa, too," Caleb added.

"I didn't know. Are you sure you're a gunsmith?" the man asked again.

Caleb tried not to show irritation. "John Parker and my Pa taught Tom and me both. Hard to say who was better at it."

"I heard Tom Parker built a special repeater. You know anything about it?" There was a hint of contempt in his voice.

Caleb went into the shop and emerged with the carbine. "Would you like a demonstration?"

"Yes," the man answered,

"I'll get us something to shoot at," Caleb said as he walked around to the wood shed. He picked up several small pieces of kindling. He silently walked up the slope and placed six sticks in the ground. Returning to where the man stood, Caleb raised the carbine to his shoulder. The first three shots clipped the wood in half, but the fourth missed by inches. His next three shots hit the remaining pieces.

"Pretty handy with that gun," the man said.

"Years of practice," said Caleb without emotion.

"Were you with Tom Parker when he died?"

"He and I both went up Culp's Hill. Brought his body back. Buried him over there," Caleb answered as he reloaded the gun. He walked back up the slope and placed six more sticks in the partially frozen earth. When he again reached the place where the man stood, Caleb offered the carbine to him. "Want a try?"

The man nodded. He raised the carbine and took careful aim. His first shot was wide and high by more than a foot. The second found its mark. Like the first, the third and fourth were misses. Finally, he got the hang of the sights and quickly dispatched the remaining targets without a miss.

"I'll buy it," he said.

Caleb replied, "It's not for sale. Make you one though. Adjust the length of the stock to fit you better."

"How much?" he asked.

"Twenty dollars," Caleb answered.

Surprised, the man offered fifteen. Caleb shook his head. "Twenty." The deal was struck.

"I'd like to know who I'm doing business with," Caleb said.

"Thomas Lenoir," the man answered.

Caleb recognized the name. Thomas Lenoir was the oldest son and namesake of Colonel Thomas Lenoir, a hero of the War of 1812. He managed the Den, a large but less than elegant estate in Haywood County.

Colonel Lenoir had died in 1861 at age 80. Rufus, his youngest son, managed the main plantation, called Fort Defiance, in Caldwell County. The middle son, Walter, had served in the Confederate army, returning as an amputee the previous May. Caleb thought little of the Lenoir family because they were slaveholders. Since the Colonel's death, the brothers had managed the sixty some slaves inherited from their father.

Lenoir seemed to read his thoughts, "My brothers and I are uncomfortable with the human part of our inheritance. I knew who you were, but I was afraid that if I told you my name, you might not show me the weapon. You enjoy a considerable reputation."

"My father was a slave," Caleb replied. "John Parker helped him earn his freedom. Seeing slaves discomforts me. I hope that those who own them show the same consideration."

Thomas Lenoir seemed taken aback by Caleb's frankness. "You speak like an educated man."

"John's wife, Susan, taught all of us to read and write. Her

Pa was a teacher. She told us that education couldn't be taken away," Caleb said. "Being free, there was no law against teaching us."

"Folks round here know it?" Lenoir asked.

"Mostly. Long as we stay away from the slaves, they let us be."

"You may not know," Lenoir said, "but we sold our slaves privately after my father's estate was settled. Most who work my farm are paid wages. We've kept some slaves, of course. Eventually, we'll sell them all."

Lenoir caught Caleb off guard. "You favor secession?"

"It's our right," Thomas answered.

"You're against slavery and for secession?" Caleb asked, confused.

"My family has different opinions. The Colonel thought that slave family ties were important. Christian reasons," Thomas said. "My brother, Walter, and his wife believe it is an evil. James Gwyn, my sister's husband, gets joy from profit in the trade."

Caleb was leery. Lenoir was talking with him as a man, not as a black man. Few white men he'd known had ever done that. Lenoir asked, "You want to know what I think?" He saw the barely perceptive nod.

"Like your father's master, I was burdened with slaves by my father. My holdings depend on those slaves. The plantations all over the South depend on them. And so does your business. Slaves should be freed, yes, but the owners must be paid for their costs. If not, our whole economy is destroyed."

"Then why not let them earn freedom, like my father did?"

Lenoir sighed. "They'd be too old. Never could earn enough. For me, the best way out was to sell. Did it privately to keep families together. Auction's too risky."

Caleb nodded. After they concluded their business, and

Lenoir returned to the Den, Caleb went over the conversation in his mind. He was unconvinced by Lenoir's words. The man seemed to be profiting from the increasing slave trade in the mountains at the same time he was professing a dislike of slavery. His attitude was like many others: slaves were children in his care. However, Caleb could not help but be caught up by the respect Lenoir had shown him.

Caleb engaged George to help make the parts for the new carbine. For the stock he used a piece of walnut that he had purchased in Asheville in October. It was good wood with a dark and beautiful grain. Once sanded, stained, and polished, it would be eye-catching.

Lenoir returned in January with his brother Walter. The empty sleeve in his jacket was evidence of his military experience. Caleb did the test firing, then adjusted the sights and opened the works for further modifications.

When the gun was reassembled, Caleb fired it again. Thomas was eager to fire it himself, so Caleb handed him the carbine. Lenoir hit ten of twelve targets on the first try. "Better than your own," he declared.

"Built to suit you," Caleb replied.

"My brother tells me you're a fine craftsman," Walter said. "I agree with him."

"Thank you," Caleb replied.

"Heard you was at Gettysburg. Fight any others?" Walter asked.

"Tom and me was at Perryville with militia. Later on at Chancellorsville. Better off here making tools and guns," Caleb said off-handedly. The fact of it being Yankee militia was hard to conceal, but he had to keep up the pretense.

"Had my share, too," Walter said glancing at his empty sleeve. "Should have listened to Nealy and my brothers. Nealy's my wife," he added.

Thomas was preoccupied with the carbine. "Fine weapon. Do you have the ammunition?"

Caleb handed Lenoir a box with 100 rounds. Thomas gave him the ten dollar balance plus payment for the ammunition. Thanking Caleb for his work, he and Walter left. It would be eighteen months before they met again.

Life in the South during 1864 and 1865 was hard and dangerous. Many still believed that somehow the Confederacy would secure its independence. Their belief was unfounded.

Union soldiers who escaped from Andersonville Prison passed through Haywood and Buncombe counties, seeking help from any Negro they encountered. The Parkers refused them. Even in the face of the coming defeat, they remained loyal to the Confederate cause.

Slaves who helped the Yankees escape hoped for protection for their own flight. When caught escaping, slaves suffered merciless punishment or were killed outright. Yankee soldiers who were caught found themselves in the Asheville or Waynesville jail or back at Andersonville.

Sherman's success in Georgia and Sheridan's in the Shenandoah Valley brought further despair among Southerners. Lincoln's re-election in the fall of 1864 was seen as sealing their doom. Businesses in the towns and villages advertised goods for sale from their existing stock as if nothing would change. The truth was that roads and rail transportation were collapsing. Grain and salt, precious commodities, were in short supply.

Expecting the worst, Susan had hoarded supplies since the first raid on their farm. As conditions worsened, she conserved more vigorously. Their supplies now were well hidden.

Blacksmithing profits dwindled to nothing. There was a large demand for the work, because so many blacksmiths were in the army, but no one could pay in other than worthless Confederate money. The shortage of raw material hindered them as well.

Taxes were another problem. North Carolina levied a ten percent flat tax on all production. Through this tax, Governor Vance managed to get relief for the poor and for the families of dead and disabled soldiers. Susan and the girls were eligible, but Sissy and her family were not since both her boys were home and able-bodied.

Pressed into home guard service because they were freemen under the age of forty-six, Caleb and George worked less and less at the forge. George proved himself almost as able with a gun as his older brother. They tracked down Union soldiers or responded to lawless acts by pro-Union supporters. It was dangerous work and placed the two men in an awkward position.

Caleb's greatest worry was retaliation. Unionist might strike the Parker farm, believing he was a traitor. Confederate supporters could attack out of resentment for their success as free coloreds. In the face of so much suffering by the soldiers' families, he saw this as the greater risk.

The war at home had turned even more vicious than it was three years earlier. Name calling and fistfights were replaced with murder and arson. Men were beaten and tortured before being killed. Bodies disappeared and were never found for proper burial. Old grudges became excuses for bushwhacking and terrorism. Unionists, smelling a Federal victory, emerged again in strength. Antagonized by years of repression, they launched new and cowardly attacks on Confederate homesteads.

The church was divided, too. Union loyalists were banished from attending services. Where were the Christian attitudes that had been preached? There seemed to be no room for forgiveness.

Something Caleb didn't realized spared the Parkers. Thomas' Legion had killed Goldman Bryson in October 1863. The Legion, including twenty-five Cherokee scouts, chased Bryson into his home territory in Cherokee County. All of Bryson's men who knew the ties Tom and Caleb had to Unionism were now prisoners or dead. Their families had fled north.

As a result, no one who knew the real story of Tom and Caleb's flight to East Tennessee could tell the tale. Their service in the Confederate army and Caleb's support for the home guard provided the Parkers with adequate protection from Unionist guerrillas. Rumors remained, but the events of the winter of 1865 would finally lay them to rest.

11

WAR'S CONSEQUENCES

The threat to the Parker homestead came from an unexpected source. Mistakenly believing that the North Carolina high landers would welcome Union troops, George Kirk again invaded the state. Kirk had heard about several mutinies of Confederate units. The best known was the insubordination of a cavalry company attached to the 69th North Carolina. They refused the orders of two successive commanding officers, James Henry and George Tait.

As an outsider sent by Governor Vance, Tait never had the support of his men. One evening they attacked him, hit him on the forehead with a rock, and effectively forced his resignation. Following the incident, the company dispersed and many hid in the mountains. Kirk failed to realize that these acts brought the mountain families closer together in support of the war. Dislike of a Confederate officer did not mean they were pro-Union.

Kirk and his 600-man force entered Haywood County from Newport, Tennessee, in February 1865. The home guard was called out to scout his movements. Caleb and George rode out with them in spite of pleas to stay home from Sissy and Melinda.

The scouts quickly determined that they were badly out-numbered and sent for reinforcements. Meanwhile, they contented themselves with sniping at Kirk's men from a safe distance.

Kirk's advance was swift, in spite of the efforts to slow him down. His men were Union regulars with defined military and political objectives. They swept into Waynesville, freed Unionists and Confederate deserters from jail, and burned the jail. Not satisfied with their success, they burned the home of James R. Love, a Confederate leader. Love's grandfather, Robert Love, had been a hero of the American Revolution.

Then they went out into the countryside. As in the Shelton Laurel Raid, the men pillaged and burned farms and homes. The Parker farm was right in Kirk's path. Finally, they stopped for the night. The home guards knew Kirk's location and would exploit the weaknesses of their position.

The home guards planned to fire at Kirk from several directions and slowly converge into a single line that would throw the Yankees backwards. Seasoned troops might have met with success. Home guards facing an experienced force had no chance at all.

It was nearing nightfall when they counterattacked. The night attack initially went as planned. Caleb's mind was flooded with memories of Culp's Hill as they moved into position around Kirk's encampment. "Stay with me and stay out of the firelight," Caleb cautioned George as they gained a line of fire on Kirk's men. "Don't give them a clear shot at you."

"Plan on living," George replied. "Too many of us Parkers dead already."

Caleb fired and wounded two Yankees before they were able to reach their weapons. George shot the same private twice. His first shot hit the man's hand and sent his tin mug sailing into the air. The second shot struck him in the chest. They both moved to the right to avoid drawing a massive volley in their direction.

The home guards fired several volleys from the trees and darkness. They had the advantage of surprise and created some disorder among the Yankees. It did not last long. Kirk's men formed a double line, fired several volleys, and proved that they would not be intimidated. Within twenty minutes, Kirk's men drove off the reinforced, but poorly trained and inexperienced, home guard.

Their attack was a success in an unintended way. Kirk abandoned plans to go farther eastward. He decided instead to return to Tennessee as quickly as possible. Caleb, George, and the home guards pursued at a safe distance until they could join forces with Confederates from all over the southwest counties. Kirk was thirteen miles northwest of Waynesville when he was ambushed again.

"Those Yankee boys are bouncing wherever we pushes them!" George exclaimed gleefully as they fired at will from concealed positions.

"Be careful, little brother," Caleb cautioned. "It can get deadly in the blink of an eye." As if to reinforce Caleb's point, a hailstorm of bullets whistled around them. Instinctively, Caleb looked in George's direction. He was all right except for some dirt that had flown up in his eyes.

Again Kirk withdrew. He and his men headed due west along Soco Creek with the intent of slipping through the mountains and into Tennessee through Soco Gap. Colonel Stringfield, a battalion of Thomas' Legion, and two dozen Cherokee Indians were waiting to greet them. The home guard continued to harass the tail of Kirk's column.

The Battle of Soco Creek was little more than a skirmishing that lasted about an hour. Both sides had about an equal number of men, and neither could gain the tactical advantage. In the end, Kirk was able to escape by maneuvering his forces for a quick dash across the mountains.

Caleb spent most of that hour making sure that George didn't commit a foolish act of bravery. It was impossible to teach his brother everything that he had learned in a year of fighting. There were tricks to staying alive. A man could only learn these tricks by watching the mistakes of others. Caleb was relieved when they started back home.

The invasion was over, but the damage had been done. Returning home, Caleb and George found their family intact, but the farm had almost been destroyed. The center posts of both barns had been ripped out and the roofs had collapsed. Susan's house and the blacksmith's shop had been set afire. It would be two months before the buildings would be restored to normal.

Susan and the girls moved in with Sissy. The women of the church protested that they shouldn't live with coloreds. Susan replied, "Sissy and I have cooked in each other's kitchens for nearly thirty years. When the winters were cold, our families always slept together in the warmest house. This Yankee deviltry is not changing that."

Fixing Susan's house came first. The fire had damaged the kitchen before the women could put it out. They scrubbed the scorched walls, floors, and ceiling. George made a new table and chairs, crude compared to those their grandfathers had built, but serviceable. Women from the church gave them new table linens and curtains. The gift was a genuine sacrifice that went toward repaying Susan's generosity over the past years.

The barns were usable enough in spite of the roof damage. Several older men from Waynesville came to help replace the center supports. Those who were able helped patch the holes. As Lee surrendered at Appomattox Court House in April, Caleb and George finished repairing the second roof.

All the while Susan bragged that the Yankees got nothing

from them. Try as they might they couldn't find her stores of supplies. Her good fortune was that they were in too much of a hurry to make a thorough search, but she was confident that her cold dry-cellars and well-hidden, watertight barrels were effective.

A shiver of fear ran through the farm when they learned that Union General Stoneman was riding through the counties nearest the Virginia border in the final months of the war. Stoneman was reinforced by Kirk. Both were under strict orders not to destroy property. He burned the Boone jail, thus destroying most of the Watauga County records. Rufus Patterson's cotton mill in Caldwell County was also destroyed.

Stoneman turned north into Virginia to concentrate on disrupting the railroads as Lee retreated. April turned to May and brought the beginning of planting season. It also brought Corporal John Singleton of Company F of the 25th North Carolina back to Haywood County.

Singleton was Annie Parker's intended beau. He had been wounded at the Crater, but was unable to come home until he had recovered from his injuries. Annie cried when she saw him. He was completely confused as a result of the stress of war and the slaughter he had seen. He had forgotten their intentions. Once home, he quickly improved, and the third Sunday after his return, they sat together in church.

Melinda's secret love also was revealed. Now that he was free, Jebediah, a house slave from Waynesville, courted her openly. The marriage was performed in June. The same week that John Singleton married Annie in September, Melinda announced she was pregnant. Only Maggy remained single.

Life on the farm became increasingly complex. The cows could no longer graze in the open lands because of new restrictive laws passed by the state legislature, now dominated by Republicans. Without this additional space, the farm could support only one-third of the herd. Land that was used to raise crops would have to be abandoned, or most of the cows would have to be sold.

With the soldiers returning, many blacksmith shops were re-opened in Waynesville. Local farmers and those who lived in the town stopped coming to the shop, confirming a change in attitudes toward the Parkers. People looked at Susan with a disdain she did not understand.

George found low-paying work with one of the revived blacksmith shops. Caleb considered finding like employment and went to Waynesville to ask around. He ran into Thomas Lenoir.

"How would you like to work for me?" he asked. "George, too. I'll pay you fair. If no one else has the brains to see your talent, I do."

Caleb answered without hesitation. "Sure would. Can't say for George. I'd be surprised if he didn't."

Lenoir arranged for their forge and shop to be moved to the Den, explaining to Caleb and George that he intended to expand his operations. Because he had not been in the Confederate service, he had opportunities not available to others. Reconstruction barred ex-Confederates from holding public office and curtailed many other privileges. The result was severe economic hardship for many who had been among the wealthy or middle class. Only the Welches, who collaborated with George Kirk, provided any competition for Lenoir.

Lenoir also decided to buy the Parker farm, with two stipulations. The first was that the Parker's cattle would be able to graze on lands owned by the Lenoir family. His second was that the Parkers would give twenty percent of what they grew to help support the Lenoir household.

In exchange, Thomas promised to provide field hands to make sure that the farm was as productive as possible. Through this arrangement, Lenoir should be able to sell most of their crops. For Susan, the arrangement was a blessing.

She opened an evening school with Sissy and Maggy for recently freed slaves and their children. Maggy liked teaching, but confided to her mother that she preferred white children.

Her revelation shocked Susan. "Margaret Lynn, you've known Sissy and her family all your life. Why don't you enjoy teaching the coloreds? There's no difference."

"Melinda and George are different, Momma. They're family. These coloreds are dirty and talk bad."

"With education, they'll get better," Susan said. "That's exactly why I'm doing this. It's our missionary duty. How else will they get on in this world?"

Maggy shook her head and said, "Can't explain it. It's just the way I feel."

When they went into Waynesville the next week, no one noticed when Maggy slipped away to mail more than a dozen letters seeking a position as a nanny or schoolmistress.

Caleb and George spent several nights each week at the Den. Some nights the weather was good enough for them to go home. George would have gone, but Caleb insisted on staying. One night George learned why: Caleb had fallen in love.

The discovery was accidental. When George unexpectedly returned to the shop for his pipe, he came upon Caleb talking with someone near the women's quarters.

"Evening, Miss Poppy," he said. "Hello, Caleb." Even in the darkness, George could sense Caleb's embarrassment.

Poppy smiled. "Evening, George. Decided to spy upon your brother?"

"Not at all," George answered. "Forgot my pipe."

"You wasn't a bit curious why Caleb stays out at night?" Poppy said. "I never took you for a fool."

"Ain't no fool," George replied indignantly. "I had half a

suspicion. Good evening. Got to get that pipe."

"That boy's got the worst timing," Caleb said when George was out of earshot. "Well, can I talk with your momma or not?"

"Except for a once-in-a-while cigar, you don't smoke. That's tolerable. Know you don't drink and you're God-fearing," she began. "You confessed about fighting."

Caleb was impatient. "I can tell your momma all that."

"Already has," Poppy interrupted with a smile.

Caleb gazed at her. She was the most beautiful woman he had ever seen. Almost as tall as he, she was darker. Ebony, they called it. No white blood in her at all. She was barely nineteen, six years younger, but she seemed already wise. Not like those silly girls.

"Please, don't tease me," he pleaded. "Let me ask your momma."

"It's your directness bothers me, Caleb Parker. And no patience neither," she replied. "You can ask my momma though. My answer's already yes."

So was her mother's. The wedding was held two weeks later, just ten days before Christmas, at the Parker's Methodist church. Her pastor, Lewis Welsh, performed the ceremony. Thomas arranged for them to have a small, ramshackle house on the plantation. Caleb was given the time to make it a proper place for them to live.

When the house was ready, they moved in. As he lay in bed with her for the first time, he felt the smoothness of her back. "You never got whipped?" he asked.

"Seen slaves whipped when I was in the other place. Momma paddled me with a spoon a couple times. Hurt so much I figured I wouldn't do anything stupid enough to get whipped. Since I got bought by Massuh Thomas, I never seen a slave whipped here," she said.

It pleased Caleb to know that. He still had his doubts about

Thomas Lenoir. The man treated his nigrahs right, but some-how not quite like the Parkers did. The thought passed as he turned his attention to Poppy. He'd never lain with a woman, nor she with a man. Awkwardly, they learned together.

"What are you thinking?" Poppy asked afterward.

"About children."

Poppy was puzzled. "What about children?"

"I name the boys. You name the girls. Seems fair to me."

"You go to sleep, Caleb," she said, "Plenty of time later for naming babies."

That same night the Teague Band struck. This group of renegades began to terrorize blacks and Republicans. One man was lynched and another was savagely whipped, both as their wives and children looked on.

After that, Lenoir warned all the coloreds not to leave the plantation without a white person to watch over them. They took his warning seriously. The Teagues weren't the only dan-ger. Many former Confederates were angry about the Yankee invasion.

Their anger was compounded by the lack of work available, the new freedoms given to former slaves, and their own loss of influence over local affairs. They directed their anger at Union-ists, Republicans, nigrahs, and anyone else who could be held accountable for their misery.

The owners of large farms and plantations, who had no war affiliations, found ways to survive. Sharecropping, after selling out to the large landowners, was one way. Other, more entre-preneurial mountain residents exploited the cool summers by attracting tourists. Unfortunately, only those who could afford to retreat to the mountains in the summer were carpetbaggers. These tourists were perfect targets for the Teagues and their fellow malcontents.

Businessmen sought help from the state soon after the war. A narrow Republican majority provided what little support it could. Federal military protection in the mountains was scarce. The larger military presence was saved for the cities and largest towns. Even Asheville had little in the way of a military occupation. The larger presence was made up of politicians, bureaucrats, and other scoundrels. Haywood County was effectively on its own.

Poppy and Caleb had little reason to leave the safety of the Den. Caleb occasionally rode the two miles to Waynesville for supplies, usually with Thomas Lenoir. Other whites would accompany them if it seemed necessary.

Susan and Sissy always traveled together even before and during the war. It suited them and their habit didn't change. George risked riding alone only when the entire trip could be accomplished in daylight. Everyone in the Negro community understood the danger. War had made things worse for coloreds, not better.

It was only nine months after the war had ended. Many wounds were open and raw. Others had festered for years. An infection was spreading. It was a sickness that would last a long time.

Christmas brought the news that a couple in Wilmington needed a nanny who also could school their seven-year-old son and five-year-old daughter. They wanted Maggy to arrive immediately after New Year's Day. Susan and Sissy took her to the train station for the long hugs good-bye. Maggy would never hug her mother again.

12

NORTHERN MIGRATION

January 1866 brought heavy snows and despair. Food was scarce, but still available for a price. The poor suffered and poverty bred a greater desire for revenge.

A thaw with sunshine brightened the last week in the month. George, who had spent the last three weeks with Caleb and Poppy, went to visit his mother and Susan to see how they had survived the cold and snow. The two women were eager to start teaching again. Running the school had become almost an obsession with them. At their insistence, George gathered more children and returned with them to the makeshift schoolhouse.

About eight o'clock that night, a man and two women from the Den arrived to escort the children home. George was torn between staying at home and returning to the plantation. He decided to go back to Caleb's house. Poppy had been stewing a chicken earlier in the afternoon.

Sissy and Susan were making do with whatever was at hand. "Can't teach and cook too," Sissy told George. "You go have supper with your brother." George didn't need any more encouragement than that. He went back to the Den when the children left.

The two women went over the events of the day as they ate their supper.

"They've been teaching each other," Susan said. "The little ones are reading better."

Sissy smiled. "And the older ones got better by being the teachers for awhile. Want some butter with that bread?"

"Yes, Michael's doing better with his addition, too. Bet Laura helped. She's sweet on him."

"Who wouldn't be? He's a charmer," said Sissy with a laugh.

"Think the missionary society will come by tomorrow?"

Sissy took a sip of coffee and a bite of soft cheese. "Not sure. My bet is on the Ethiopian Ladies of Haywood."

"Won't take that bet. Our luck is they'll both show up. We'll be tripping over each other," Susan said.

The sudden sound of hoofbeats startled them.

"Now who would that be?" Sissy stood up and walked toward the door. "Coming up fast." She pushed aside the curtain. A single gunshot rang out. Sissy fell flat on her back. Blood flowed from a hole below her throat. Susan, frozen in terror, heard only a gasp before Sissy fell silent.

Another shot was fired. Shock and fear propelled Susan away from the front of the house. She heard the sound of breaking glass in the back room. Glancing behind her, Susan saw a flaming torch and smelled smoke. Two more fireballs came through the front windows. She screamed.

Somehow she was on the front porch, holding onto the railing to keep from falling. She could make out at least eight horsemen silhouetted in the snow-covered yard.

"Stop teaching them niggers!" someone yelled.

"Never!" she cried. She saw the muzzle flashes and tried to dodge them. A bullet hit her in the hip and the another in the shoulder. Seeing her collapse, the guerrillas rode off.

Susan lay still on the porch, consumed in pain. "Sissy," she whispered. "Sissy, where are you?" Behind her she heard the popping of the fire as it spread from room to room. With a wordless prayer for strength, she dragged herself away from the burning house. Then she fainted.

The flames were a beacon clearly seen from a distance of at least a mile. When neighbors reached the farm, they knew there was no saving the house. Susan was taken to Sissy's house and her wounds tended to. As word spread, George, Caleb, and Poppy arrived. John and Annie didn't get there until shortly after daybreak.

Susan was weak, but conscious. The doctor thought she might survive. She pulled Caleb close to her. "Did you get Sissy out?" she asked, her voice a hoarse whisper.

"No, ma'm," he said. "Not yet. Still too hot in there." She saw the grief in his face and turned away.

"Damn them!" she burst out. *"Damn them to hell!"*

For the next two days, Susan appeared to recover. She wanted to hear about Sissy's burial service and seemed to relax when she heard Sissy was at rest next to Jonah. "Soon I'll be with John again," she said, "and away from this vicious, never-ending war."

The next morning she showed signs of congestion. Her fever rose and it was clear that pneumonia had set in. By the end of the week she was dead.

Standing by the coffin before the church service began, Caleb said, "I'm leaving North Carolina. No reason to stay now."

John Singleton broke the silence. "If Annie agrees, so are we."

"That I do," said Annie in support of her husband. "What about you, George?"

George didn't answer. He was still reeling from his mother's murder. If only he had stayed that night. . . .

"I want to kill the bastards," he said. "But if I try, they'll kill me, too. Might as well go with y'all."

It was decided quickly. They would keep their plans quiet. Their destination would be Pittsburgh. Singleton had spent nearly two years there before the war. He knew people there and liked the area. Caleb, Poppy, and George agreed to head north with John and Annie. Melinda and Jeb wanted to go only as far as Virginia.

Taking care of the family's funds was another matter needing attention. Everyone in the family knew where the barrel-and-barn money was hidden. Only Caleb knew about the dry cellar safe. Annie agreed to go with him to recover what was left.

She followed him into the ruins of Susan's house. They made their way through burnt timbers and scorched furniture. Caleb kicked away a charred braid rug by the back wall in the far corner of Susan's bedroom. Carefully, he pried back a piece of molding to expose the hinges of a trap door. "Susan showed this to Tom and me a long time ago. It may be empty now."

He lifted up the corners of the door with his knife. It took some effort, but the nails gave way and the door was raised to expose a narrow stairway into a small stone cellar. The room was barely five feet square and not much higher. "This is where your grandfather kept his money," he told Annie.

She couldn't see anything but stone walls. "You sure?" she asked.

"Not sure anything's here now. Gotta look for that safe none the same."

"We have quite a bit already," Annie said as Caleb began searching for loose stones.

"Your grandfather kept his moonshine in here, too. Just kicked an old jug. Go get a candle from my mama's house, would you?" She hustled off.

When she returned, she passed the lit candle to Caleb and could see five good-sized bags on the floor. Caleb retrieved two more. They carried them together back to Sissy's house. Most of the money came from thirty years of saving by John's father. The rest was money that John had saved over another twenty-five years.

"There's more," Caleb announced. "My pa had an identical cellar built under his bedroom. The barrel-and-barn money was for everyday. This is children's money—for us, if we ever needed it."

Annie said, "We all get equal shares."

Jonah had saved two bags of mostly silver coin. John Singleton didn't understand why George, Melinda, and Caleb got equal shares with them. Annie was firm. "Folks didn't know that this was a family business. Two Parker families are one. Have been since Jonah paid off his and Sissy's freedom."

"How'd a smith make so much money?" John asked.

Caleb tried to explain. "Blacksmith, gunsmith, cooper, wheelwright, and furniture maker. Whatever it took, we did. Before the war, we had six men working for wages. We made a profit off their work. Didn't need no slaves. Didn't want none neither."

Caleb and George still had to face Thomas Lenoir. It was not just a matter of telling him they were leaving. Their agreement stated that Lenoir owned the property outright if they left. His response surprised Caleb.

"I can't protect you here," he said. "Your mother and Susan were fine women. You boys do good work. Better you do it elsewhere and stay alive. I'll miss you. Good thing you're riding with Singleton, though. Safer."

"Singleton won't stop them," George said, barely disguising his contempt.

Lenoir sensed George's anger. "If you're leaving here, they won't bother you. It's staying that makes them hate you. Before the war, there were more than a quarter of a million free Negroes in the South, 30,000 in North Carolina alone. Most stayed home. A few went with the army to practice their trade. 'Course they got mixed in with slaves that drove wagons and cooked. Others went North and fought with the Yankees."

"I saw plenty who fought with the South," Caleb interjected. "Some regiments with Jackson had maybe one soldier in fifteen who was colored."

"There were," Lenoir replied. "About 3,000 in Jackson's Corps. Yankees knew it 'cause that rabble rouser Frederick Douglass complained to Lincoln himself."

Caleb was trying to be respectful. "I don't understand your point. They were free, like me. We fought to protect our homes, just like whites did."

"Some folks thought this war was about slavery. By 1863, Yankees made it so. I didn't hold with that. Now, with the slaves being free, all coloreds are the same. Don't matter that some were free before. Y'all are seen as the reason for Southern misery. A couple generations, those like you who fought for the cause will be forgotten. A generation after that will deny that *any* nigruhs were soldiers in the Confederate army."

Caleb was content with Lenoir's approval. They asked Poppy's mother if she'd come along, but she refused. Sad as she was to lose her daughter, she did nothing to discourage the move, easing Poppy's distress at leaving her behind.

They had to find a way to hide their money for the trip. Raiders and guerrillas were everywhere. The men put coins inside their belts, using two strips of leather instead of a single strap. Hidden cuffs at the bottom of their pants provided another place. A zigzag pattern near the hem of the women's skirts kept even more coins.

They couldn't wear all their money. It was too heavy. They needed many hiding places—false bottoms in their handbags held most of the remaining funds; hidden compartments on the wagons held the rest.

After a week of preparation, they were ready to leave. The men carried Parkers and a sidearm. Caleb gave Tom's carbine to John Singleton so that the weapon would stay with Tom's side of the Parker clan. George and Jeb had duplicates made at the same time that Caleb had produced the weapon for Thomas Lenoir. John and Jonah's Parker carbines were gifts to the Lenoirs.

The family began their journey by going through Asheville and over the mountains into Virginia. Unlike Caleb's return from Gettysburg with the two-wheeled cart, the journey using sturdier wagons was half again faster. Going north down the Shenandoah Valley on the pike was rapid.

Jeb and Melinda turned east at Manassas Gap and eventually settled in Rockville, Maryland. From Manassas Gap, John and Annie, Caleb and Poppy, and George continued on through Harper's Ferry, across Maryland, and into Pennsylvania. They arrived in Pittsburgh on February 28. Deep snow still covered the ground. All the Parkers could see why Singleton loved the area. The river and the mountains were as beautiful as at home.

John's friends welcomed Annie like family. Caleb, Poppy, and George were received with little more than polite cordiality. George didn't care. He found work immediately in a small foundry. The active social community welcomed him. Pittsburgh gave George an opportunity to be the man he wanted to be. The fact that several young women found him attractive added to his pleasure.

Caleb could have taken a job in the same foundry where George worked. He didn't. There were too many people there for his taste. It reminded him of being with the army. Plenty of jobs were available in Pittsburgh, even with all of the soldiers returning home. New buildings were going up everywhere.

Caleb finally found a job in a small shop, but the pay was paltry.

The crowded city was not home to him. The air was foul. He wanted the countryside. Poppy agreed with him No one was surprised when after only a month they said that they'd like to go farther north. How much farther they didn't know.

Leaving Pittsburgh, Caleb and Poppy followed the mountains north, while remaining on the flat lands to the east. It was a difficult ride. The roads were muddy and hard to traverse as the early spring thaw began. The farms in western Pennsylvania were not like those Caleb had seen as the Confederate army marched toward Gettysburg. They were not as neat, more like the farms at home.

"Why not turn back and see if we can find a home around Gettysburg?" Poppy asked.

"Cain't do it. Too many bad memories."

Poppy understood very well, but she wanted to settle down. She was after a home, not adventure. "What *do* you want, Caleb?"

"My own shop again. Somewhere being a colored man makes no difference."

"Think the Yankees'll give you that?

Caleb didn't have an answer. It was the puzzlement that had bothered him since the war began. "Reckon I don't know. Surely didn't see better in Pittsburgh. We'll know when we find it."

"We gonna go all the way to Canada?"

"No," he answered sharply. "We'll find a place sooner than that."

"I'm mighty tired of riding in this wagon."

At the next small town, he found a place to hitch the horses. They walked along the street looking for a place to buy more provisions. The general store wasn't twenty-five yards from where they left the wagon.

"You fixing on staying here?" the shopkeeper asked as Caleb paid for the items they selected.

"Depends on if you need a blacksmith," he said evenly.

"Sure don't. You be on your way. Don't need you here."

"Fraid we gotta ride some more," Caleb said when they got back to the wagon."

Poppy smiled. "Be glad to leave this place. It sure ain't hospitable."

They spent that night wrapped in each other's arms. The fire in front of them was warm. Even better, the town was ten miles behind them. "We'll find someplace yet," Caleb said. Poppy snuggled closer and they fell asleep.

Rain started to fall at dawn the following morning. By noon it was a torrential downpour. Caleb found a stand of trees with enough of a clearance for the wagon. Pulling off the road, they intended to hole up there until the storm ended.

Making a tent within the wagon was more difficult in the heavy rain. He worried about the horses getting the fungus from standing in the ankle-deep water and the mud. He noted higher, drier ground nearby. Tethering them there and stretching a canvas to cover them, Caleb was satisfied that they were safe.

Inside the tent, Poppy had made room for them and a picnic of crackers, cheese, and dried fruit, along with the apple cider they bought in town. They took the time to be lazy, something they hadn't done.

"We need to talk about where we going," Poppy said softly.

"North."

"Not good enough. You got a plan. Tell me now."

Caleb shifted uneasily to sit up cross-legged. He knew what he didn't want and that was another city. What he wanted he wasn't sure he could say. "I'm looking for a Waynesville without the new meanness."

"That died about ten years ago."

"How can you be so sure? You was still a slave on the coast then."

"Ain't the point and you know it. You got a plan or we gonna be the new children of Israel?"

Caleb smiled. "This ain't no desert, woman. Besides, after forty years of wandering, we be dead."

Laughing, she punched him in the arm. "Sweet Jesus, husband, you any idea where we're headed?"

"I'm thinking we might find a nice town in New York."

"Mountains getting smaller the farther north we go."

"People is what counts."

She let the conversation end there, but Caleb took her feelings to heart. Somewhere they must find a place they would feel at home.

13

CUBA & RUSHFORD

They crossed into New York and turned east of Jamestown, avoiding the larger towns. The smaller villages needed Caleb's skills, so he found occasional work. Payment for his services was meager and was often in food instead of cash.

The lack of cash payment concerned Caleb because he wanted to conserve his savings. Poppy was sure that she was pregnant. It was, he knew, the reason for her insistence on settling down as soon as possible.

West of Olean, they came upon the owner of a small farm. "Got any work needs doing?" Caleb asked, trying to pronounce his words as clearly as a Northerner would. "I'm a smith."

"Plenty," the farmer answered. "A smith, you say?"

"Yes," Caleb answered, "Gunsmith, blacksmith, and some wood work, too."

"Gunsmith?" the farmer repeated. "The hammer spring on my rifle's broke. Taking it to town would cost me a whole day's work."

Caleb fixed the old rifle in about an hour. Three days later, after a dozen odd jobs, he had five more dollars in his pocket. He also had preserves, corn meal, a smoked ham, and canned vegetables. The greater gifts, however, were directions to other farms that needed his services.

It took them more than three weeks to go another forty miles. Even though he had plenty of work, Caleb knew they needed a permanent place to live. Poppy couldn't continue to ride in the wagon. Their path turned northeast into Cuba in late April.

In town, Caleb learned that there were three men looking for him. Two were blacksmiths. The third, Russell Thurston, was a gunsmith. All three offered him work. Caleb agreed to work three hours a day and Saturdays for Thurston. The rest of the time he would work for a blacksmith who provided a two-room cabin at a reasonable rent.

Thurston was interested in the Parker. Caleb told him the carbine's history. When Caleb took the Parker apart, Thurston was fascinated by the craftsmanship.

"Men from around here were in the 85th New York Volunteers," Hurston told him. "They're Plymouth Pilgrims. Know how they got that name?"

Caleb shook his head.

"The hats. Some fool issued them tall, stiff black hats like the Iron Brigade wore. Then, they got captured at Plymouth, North Carolina," Thurston continued. "April 18, 1864. Those that didn't get killed went to Andersonville. A few died in prison, but, thankfully, the war was almost over. They got paroled and came home."

"My best friend died at Gettysburg," Caleb volunteered.

"He a Negro, too?" Thurston asked.

He smiled and answered softly, "No, sir, he was white."

Thurston accepted that without comment.

Caleb and Poppy's first child was a son, named Caleb Thomas. Caleb had a job, a house, and a family, but he didn't feel like he belonged. Even though Cuba was barely a large town, it was too big. Caleb thought a smaller village might suit them better. Poppy was pregnant again. Their second son, Jonah John, would be born later that year.

During the months before Jonah was born, Caleb did some scouting around. His trips first took him up Rush Creek to Bellville and McGrawville. Both were too small to support his business. Oramel, up Crawford Creek and on the north bank of the Genesee River, also was too small. Pushing farther east, he determined that Belfast was similar to Cuba. He would have to compete with blacksmiths long known to the white community. For similar reasons, Wellsville was not considered suitable.

At the confluence of Indian Creek and Caneadea Creek, Caleb found a village called Rushford. Smaller than Cuba, Rushford was growing but lacked anyone skilled in all the trades in which Caleb was expert.

As he approached the general store, a young boy of about eleven walked up to him.

"Where are you from?" he asked.

"Cuba," Caleb answered, suprised.

"Were you a slave or something?"

Caleb smiled, then threw back his head and laughed. "Lord, no. I'm free and always have been."

The boy wrinkled up his nose. "I thought all niggers from down South were slaves. You talk funny."

"Oh, no young'n, there's free coloreds all over. Even before the war. Now, we're all free. As to talking funny, I moved here from North Carolina. To me, you're the one talks funny." Overhearing the conversation from inside, the storekeeper chuckled.

"My name's Frank, Frank Higgins," the boy said.

"And my name's Caleb, Caleb Parker."

"Nice meetin' yew, Caleb," Frank said, trying to imitate Caleb's drawl.

"Nice meeting you, too, Frank," Caleb replied trying to imitate Frank's upstate twang.

"Whatcha doing here, Caleb?"

"Just seeing if maybe Rushford could do with a smithy,"

"Haven't had one since before the war," the shopkeeper called out. "Died at Andersonville. I helped carry his body out."

"You a Plymouth Pilgrim?" Caleb asked, once inside the store.

The shopkeeper seemed surprised. "How's a Southern boy know about Plymouth Pilgrims?"

"Russell Thurston told me 'bout them."

"Good man, Russell," the shopkeeper said. "Rode with the 9th New York. Took a bullet in the leg on the last day at Gettysburg. Bought this gun from him last year," he said, laying a pistol on the counter.

That explains Russell's limp, Caleb thought to himself. "I work for Mr. Thurston. Need to strike out on my own though."

"Know what this is?"

"It's a LeMat," Caleb answered.

The shopkeeper nodded. "Russell took it off a dead Rebel. That lower barrel killed one of his mates and badly wounded two more with a single shot." Frank, who had followed Caleb into the store, was wide-eyed. "Russell killed the Reb and brought the gun home. For some reason, he didn't want to keep it. When I came in looking for a pistol, he sold it to me cheap. It's a bear of a gun to load."

A teenaged girl called for Frank. He said a quick goodbye and was gone. "The boy's father is O.T. Higgins. He owns this store and others in New York and down into Pennsylvania. Frank's mother is very ill. I don't think the boy knows she'll probably die soon," the shopkeeper said. "My name's John Ryan."

"Guess you heard, I'm Caleb Parker."

"So you're thinking about moving here?" John asked.

Caleb hesitated. "If Rushford can use me. I'd need a place to set up shop."

"O.T. owns the property the old smithy shop is on. You talk with O.T. If he'll rent it, you got a good place to work from," John said offering his hand.

Unsure of what to do, Caleb put out his own hand. John shook it vigorously. "O.T.'s up the street. Can't miss him. He's a big man and not just because of his money. You want an opportunity, O.T. is the man to see."

Caleb left the store and walked down the street. He hadn't gone far before he saw Frank again. He was standing with the teenaged girl, an older women, and a man that Caleb presumed to be O.T. Higgins.

Caleb could hear Frank say to his father, "That's the colored man I told you about. He wants to move here!" The boy's father told him to hush. Caleb stopped and waited.

"Understand you gave my boy some entertainment?" O.T. said loudly enough for Caleb to hear. "Come on closer, Frank tells me you're a blacksmith."

Caleb walked to within a few feet of the Higgins and stopped. "Blacksmith and gunsmith. I also does some wagon work, Mr. Higgins."

O.T. introduced Frank's sister Clara and the children's governess, Janette Caldwell. "Let's get into my carriage, Caleb," O.T. said.

The horse took off with a bolt, and Caleb recalled the phrase "driving like Jehu." He laughed to himself. O.T. was some go-getter. They headed to the north side of town. There, Caleb saw a sizeable blacksmith shop. Off to the back was a field some 200 yards deep that ended in dense woods.

"Do you have all the tools you'll need?" O. T. asked.

"I brought the tools I could from North Carolina. Don't

have no iron or steel. That I have to buy," Caleb answered.

"I'll arrange it on credit for you. My personal notes kept things going during the war. Don't mind helping the town out some more."

Caleb glanced at Higgins in surprise. "Don't need no credit. We saved gold and silver coin afore the war. My Pa's share came with me."

Higgins replied sharply, "That's between you and me. Not everyone would look kindly on you having that much money of your own. I judge people well and I believe you're trustworthy. Some won't look at it that way. I'll see that you get a private account at the bank in Houghton."

"Thank you, sir," Caleb responded, trying to hide the surprise in his voice.

"You'll have plenty of customers soon enough," O.T. interjected. "Then, the money you have as a merchant won't be much of a surprise."

Caleb, Poppy, and the boys were settled in Rushford by the winter of 1867. Less than a year later, on a hot August day, Lucia Higgins, O.T.'s wife, died. She had spent the early summer back East, desperately consulting with the best doctors she could find. There was no helping or saving her, so she came back to Rushford to die.

On the afternoon after she passed away, Frank, now thirteen, felt he had to get away from the grief-filled house and headed to the woods on the north side of town, toward Caleb's shop. He dragged his feet as he moved along, deep in concentration.

Caleb was at work when he heard a scream. Looking out the back window, he saw Frank running at full speed. Behind him was a pack of wild dogs. The lead dog wasn't fifteen feet away from him. Caleb reached for his carbine and took aim.

The lead dog's paws struck Frank's shoulder blades, and he fell to the ground. A bullet whizzed past his right ear. It caught the dog under his jaw, severed its backbone, and exploded out of the back of his head.

Caleb saw Frank fall and the spray of blood from the dog's skull. "Stay down, boy!" he shouted. Frank didn't move.

Caleb cocked the lever to shoot the next dog. The angle was right. Caleb's second shot struck the second dog behind the left shoulder. What remained of the pack stopped and froze. One more shot near the middle of the pack made them scamper back to the woods.

Frank couldn't get up. His heart was racing. He coughed and gasped for breath. The first dog lay dead beside him, pinning his left arm to the ground. He could hear the last whimpers of the second dog.

Suddenly, Caleb was there. "You all right boy?"

Frank nodded, still stunned. It was all he could do. Caleb stood up and ended the second dog's suffering. Rolling the dead dog off Frank's arm, Caleb helped him sit up. "Dogs don't attack people less they're starving or rabid. Even then they don't take to it much. They'd rather go after an easier kill," Caleb said. "Must not be much game out there."

Frank stood up and started breathing more easily. Caleb picked up the Parker and walked back to the shop. An image of Tom came to his mind, and his eyes filled with tears. He was glad that others had reached Frank by now. It gave him the chance to slip away.

Caleb sat on a stool and leaned back against the wall. After a while, his composure regained, he got up and went back to work. It was an easy job—wrought iron railing.

"Caleb," said a voice. Caleb looked up and saw O.T. Higgins standing in the doorway. He was shaking as if from a chill. "I couldn't stand another loss," he said in an unsteady voice.

"Another loss?" Caleb asked.

"My wife died this morning, not three hours ago."

Caleb was stunned. "I'm so sorry, Mr. Higgins. She was such a kind lady."

Higgins held up his hand as if to say that's enough. Caleb could see the redness around O.T.'s eyes. "Frank was dazed. Probably didn't even know where he was. Can't imagine why those dogs came into town like that. No matter. You, sir, saved his life. From what he told me, that was some incredible shooting."

"I was scared I'd hit the boy. Haven't shot that gun serious like in more'n four years."

"Just wanted to thank you, Caleb," Higgins said. "We'll talk again later." He turned and walked away.

The Rushford *Centennial* ran a big story, based on an interview with Frank. Caleb's name was mentioned three times. He read the story to Poppy, who seemed more impressed with Caleb's heroism than he was. The same issue included Lucia Higgins obituary.

Several weeks later, on a Saturday evening, O.T. Higgins appeared at the Parkers' doorway. Poppy invited him in.

"I should apologize," he said. "I meant to come here many days ago."

"No reason to, Mr. Higgins." Caleb said, offering him a chair.

"Please, call me O.T. Everyone else does. This isn't the South." Caleb nodded. "After you shot those dogs, I said we'd talk again." O.T. continued. "I want to give you something."

Poppy and Caleb looked at each other. Higgins said, "I don't know what to give you. I want you to tell me."

Puzzled, Caleb said, "I don't understand."

"Frank is my only son. I won't have another, and you saved his life. I can't put a price on that. At the same time, I am in your debt. What would mean the most to you?"

Caleb stood up, walked across the room, and looked out the window. "I can't take money for doing something like that. It was instinct."

"It doesn't have to be money, Caleb. I want to say thanks the best way I can."

"O.T., I know that. What's really valuable to us—and to you—is our children." Caleb gestured at the two boys playing by the fireplace.

"Is there something I can do for your children?"

Caleb leaned against the windowsill and looked Higgins straight in the eyes as he had rarely done with any white person. The two men stared at each other for more than a minute. "I know what I want, if you're willing."

Higgins nodded. Caleb continued, "I want my children educated. Miz Parker, that's Tom's mama, said education was something that could never be taken away. It's more than money, I'm talking about. I mean seeing that they get into a good school so they can amount to something special. Poppy never learned reading, writing, or ciphering. That's like working blind."

The look on Higgins' face was confusion. "Your children will be educated. That's state law. Are you asking for something different?"

"I am," Caleb said. "I can read, write, and figure, but I'm a smith 'cause it was my only choice."

"Based on what I know, you can afford more education for your boys," Higgins interjected.

Caleb stiffened. His eyes glanced at his newborn son. "Takes more than money. Besides, I don't know if what I'll have will be enough. What I need is help, your influence. If my boys want to be something, and they're smart enough to learn it, you make sure it happens."

Higgins nodded again. He understood Caleb's concern.

"Agreed. I'll see that Poppy learns to read and write, too."

Poppy clapped her hands. "Would mean a lot, sir."

They shared a glass of freshly pressed cider to commemorate the promise.

A week later, Frank left for the Review Military Academy of Poughkeepsie, New York. The following week, a tutor arrived for Poppy. As the boys grew, and more children were added, the door of the schoolhouse—and of college—was open to them.

Eventually, Caleb Thomas became a teacher. Jonah John was given the opportunity to go to college, but chose to be a blacksmith and a gunsmith like his father. Orrin Thrall, also called O.T., who was born in 1869, became a doctor. Then came Frank Wayland in 1872; he learned civil engineering. (Poppy got to name only one child, Belle Ann, who was stillborn in 1876. There were no more children.)

Frank Higgins went into business at the age of nineteen. He was cautious, conservative, and very successful. His large property interests extended to the Midwest and West Coast.

He was more than a businessman; he was also a civic leader, serving as a trustee of the Western New York Home for Friendless and Dependent Children and the Chautauqua Assembly. A Republican all his life, Frank was nominated as a senatorial candidate for the state assembly in 1893. He won in a landslide and served successive terms in 1896, 1898, and 1900. In 1902 he was elected lieutenant governor of New York, and in 1905 he became the governor. Caleb followed his progress with a deep sense of pride.

14

REUNION

After more than forty years of marriage, Caleb was alone. Poppy died in 1907. Caleb didn't know what to do with himself, so Caleb T, who taught school in Albany, insisted that his father move in with him and his wife, Eleanor.

When the governor died in the middle of his term in1908, Caleb wept. Because he was in Albany, Caleb went to the funeral. Frank had been his friend since they first met.

In late June 1913, Caleb opened up the long narrow trunk in his room. He removed the Parker and held it in his seventy-one-year-old hands. It felt heavier than he remembered. "Eight and a half pounds is still eight and a half pounds," he muttered. "Must be me getting old." Caleb gently laid the carbine on the foot of his bed.

The weathered slouch hat came out next. He placed it on his head. Standing up, he looked in the mirror to make sure it was straight. In his own eyes, Caleb was young and ready for battle. His jacket and pants followed. Removing the hat for the moment, he changed into the old clothes. The hat went back on and was straightened one more time.

Had it been fifty years?

Caleb didn't remove the gun belt. He just stared at it and gave himself the luxury of a few more memories. The carbine was returned to its place. Kneeling, he closed the trunk. He took the stairs slowly, checking his pocket for the train tickets he knew he'd picked up off the dresser.

"C.T., I'm ready to go," Caleb called out.

C.T. emerged from the kitchen. "No need to yell, Pa. I hear all right," he said, knowing the old man was a little deaf.

Eleanor rode with them to the station. Caleb embraced them both and got onto the train. Only a few other coloreds shared the car out of Albany; more got on in New York City.

When he changed trains in Philadelphia, the car was nearly full. Another older man took the seat next to Caleb. They didn't exchange greetings. The train was nearing Harrisburg when the man spoke, "Going to Gettysburg?" he asked in a New England accent.

"Yes, sir," Caleb answered.

"I was with the 54th Massachusetts," his seatmate offered.

"I was with the 23rd Virginia."

"Survived Fort Wagner," he said before the meaning of Caleb's statement registered. "You were secesh?"

"Survived Culp's Hill."

The man asked incredulously, "Why in hell would you, a Negro, fight with the Rebs?"

"Why'd you fight with the Yankees?" Caleb asked in return.

"To free the slaves, of course."

Caleb said, "I already was free. Weren't you?"

"'Course, I was," the old man said. "What about those millions who weren't?"

The question made Caleb uncomfortable, but he expected it. "Yankee cavalry murdered my father in cold blood. He was a loyal Unionist. So was the white family he and my mother worked with. I fought with the Confederacy 'cause it was my home," he answered. "What the Union did cost me my life. They destroyed everything I knew. At Culp's Hill, they killed my best friend—and he was white."

"And where do you live now?"

"With my son in Albany."

The other man settled back in the seat. The look on his face was contemptuous. "So now you live in the North among the no-good Yankees."

Caleb was irritated by his attitude. He never cared much for city folk, and this one reminded him why. "I live in the North because after the Yankees was done, I couldn't live in North Carolina or nowhere in the South no more."

"The North did nothing but keep this country together and free the slaves," was his seatmate's retort.

"You're absolutely right," Caleb began, "at least as far as that goes. How many white folks you see in this here car? Colored folks is free. That's the truth, but we aren't treated equal, no how. And slavery was horrible. I know 'cause I saw it up close. Suspect you did too."

"But you still fought for the South?" the man interrupted.

Caleb was tired of defending himself. Somehow this man couldn't understand his point of view. "Slavery is something that was," he said. "The way people treat each other still *is*. That boy who died on Culp's Hill was my brother in every way but blood."

"You really think you weren't his nigger?"

Caleb gave the man a cold stare. "Yes, I do. He'd of near kilt any man that said so, too. We started the war with Yankee militia and walked away from a northerner who didn't treat coloreds right. When we joined the 23rd, I marched, ate, slept, and fought aside the whites. The 54th was all colored troops. Am I right?"

"Except for the officers," he answered. "Where you going with this?"

"Hear me out, now. I came home after Gettysburg. Whites pretty much treated me the same 'til the war ended. Then, it got worse. White people ran me outta the South, but the Yankees in Pennsylvania didn't treat me right neither. Went all the way into New York before things got right. I knew Frank Higgins—the late governor of New York—since he was a boy. That's why I stayed. His family and that town treated me proper."

"What you trying to say? Colored folks never been treated right."

"That's what I'm telling you. Lincoln talked about some perfect Union. You and me still fighting to be a part of it," Caleb answered. "War didn't change that none. I figured some white folks treats us right and others don't. Those that do, I stick with. Those that don't, I stay away from. Main thing is, don't matter where they live, North or South."

"That's true enough of all folks, colored and white," the man said.

"You know what's ahead, but we're going there together," Caleb answered.

The man spotted someone he thought he knew and got up to join him. Caleb sat alone for the rest of the trip. When they arrived in Gettysburg, the town was crowded with old men wearing faded uniforms of blue and gray. Memories crowded his mind—awful memories, happy memories. They flickered in and out of his mind.

He wandered in the direction of the Great Camp. There were rows and rows of tents with a mess area at the end of each row. Union rows for whites. Union rows for coloreds. Confederate rows for whites. All organized by regiment, brigade, and division. The divisions were organized by corps. There were no rows for black Confederates. It was as if he'd never existed.

He searched out the 23rd Virginia. Very few of them were left among those Confederates who originally fought. Caleb

found only one man from the Richmond Sharpshooters, someone he barely knew. Captain Tompkins was not there. One man
recognized him and called to the others. "This here's the nigger
friend of that Carolina sharpshooter. Took him home after the
Yankees killed him."

"His name was Tom Parker," Caleb added.

Another man said, "That's right, Tom Parker. He had that
fancy repeater."

With that, they all remembered, too. The white Confederates of the 23rd welcomed their old comrade, giving him one of
their tents. Just like during the war fifty years earlier, he ate
with them, slept in their camp, and swapped stories with them.
When he said he lived in Albany, they all thought he meant
Georgia. He didn't correct their misunderstanding.

They walked to Culp's Hill the next morning, talking of
what happened after Gettysburg. Caleb learned of Colonel
Walton's death at Mine Run and how Major Fitzgerald stayed
with them until Appomattox.

On an impulse, Caleb stopped in front of a sketch artist in
Gettysburg who had several stands of arms nearby that he used
as props. He saw a Spencer propped against an iron rail and
picked it up. His mind went back more than half a century to
Charleston, when he talked with Tom about making a similar
gun.

"Want me to sketch you?" the artist asked. "Only two-bits."

Caleb sat down on the stool cradling the Spencer in his
arms. There he sat for more than an hour. "At my age, sitting
still comes easy. It's moving that's hard."

"How'd you manage to live so long?"

"Just get up each morning and remind myself to keep breathing," he said. The sketch was his lone treasure of the reunion.
There were commemorative medals to be bought, but Caleb
would have none of them. "There weren't no glory in killing or
dying, just surviving," was all he'd say.

Caleb Parker

For Caleb, the War Between the States ended at last during those three days. President Woodrow Wilson came to speak. He said what Caleb had tried to tell that soldier from the 54th Massachusetts. Caleb hoped that he was listening.

"These venerable men crowding here to this famous field have set us a great example of devotion and utter sacrifice. They were willing to die that the people might live. But their task is done. Their day is turned into evening. They look to us to perfect what they have established. Their work is handed unto us, to be done in another way but not in another spirit. Our day is not over; it is upon us in full tide."

The last night, they toasted their fallen comrades, and the next morning Caleb returned to Albany tired, but more enthusiastic about life than C.T. had seen him in the years since Poppy died.

The physical strain of the Gettysburg trip proved too much for the old man. Caleb died August 5, 1913, the same day forty-five years earlier that Caleb shot the wild dogs chasing Frank Higgins across the field.

We took his body back to Rushford to bury him next to Poppy and Belle Ann. John Singleton had died in 1898, but Annie, George, and Melinda came. George's wife had died the year before in a carriage accident, and Melinda's Jeb was bedridden. He died a month after Caleb's burial.

After Caleb rescued Frank, he had a new home and a family to replace the one he had lost. The Methodist Church welcomed them. Their Sunday school was the largest in the church's history—my father and his brothers attended every Sunday. Still, Caleb said he felt that he was an outsider.

He often complained that the war ended one wrong—slavery—and created three more. Freedom means nothing when it's replaced by a new kind of slavery. Owning his own business was something few other Negroes in the South did. The jobs that might have been theirs vanished when the plantation owners lost their land. What was left was sharecropping. That was almost as bad as slavery. For some it was worse.

In his mind there were two wrongs: one was against the former slaves and the other against the whites who had owned them and who were never compensated for their financial loss. But a worse wrong was being blamed, as a Negro, for the war. Caleb fought for the South because it was where he was born and raised. Carolina's mountains meant something to him. It was a home that was lost forever when the war ended. The Union meant little or nothing to him.

I know better, however, about what Caleb's family gained. I've had to put his story together from the tales he told. Annie, George, and Melinda helped with the parts he didn't or wouldn't tell. My father, C. T., and I both teach history. My grandfather's bravery and skill with that old Parker carbine won us an education. That education helped me learn enough to put this down on paper.

Caleb certainly placed a high value on the education of his children. Through his actions on one August afternoon, and the gratitude of O.T. Higgins, I got an opportunity that I otherwise might not have had. If it wasn't for the friendship of Caleb and Tom before the Civil War and Susan teaching him the value of education, Caleb never would have asked O.T. for the payment he received.

Now, as another great war lies in front of us, my children and grandchildren need to know his story before the memories of another generation of Americans take its place. They need to know that my grandfather was a reconstructed Yankee. He was a man of color who did what he thought was right for the Confederate States of America.

Caleb Thomas Parker, Jr.
Rochester, N.Y. 1914

NOTES AND ACKNOWLEDGMENTS

The 1860 Census enumerated 30,000 "free persons of color" living in North Carolina. Most of them lived in the coastal region of the state, with about one in four to one in five being slave owners. This concentration dimished as one went farther west until reaching the mountains, where very few such people could be found in each county.

In his 1886 article entitled, "The Free Negroes of North Carolina," David Dodge wrote:

> To North Carolina belongs the sorry honor of being more lenient in the execution, if not in the spirit, of her laws governing this unhappy class than either Virginia or any of the other Southern States. Not only did she contain the largest proportion of whites, Texas alone excepted, and have therefore less to fear from a servile insurrection, but the Negroes, instead of being collected on large plantations to themselves, were more generally divided up among smaller owners, in much closer contact with the whites, better understood, better treated, and consequently less disposed and less able to inflict harm.

Dodge later notes that "free Negroes" (his term) in North Carolina had the right to own property. There are, however, other facts that must be considered. Free Negroes could not travel freely, nor did they have the rights of white citizens. They could not vote nor testify in court against whites.

These restrictions were not unique to the Southern slaveholding states and were in force in the North as well. Racism in the nineteenth century was not sectional. The large cities of the northeast passed laws discriminating against the Irish and Italians; these laws also were applied to "free persons of color" residing in the North. The states of Massachusetts, Rhode Island, New York, and Pennsylvania all were complicit. Illinois, as another example, abolished slavery, but banned Negroes from emigrating into the state.

Reconstructed Yankee is historical fiction, but I attempted to be as historically accurate as possible. All of the Parkers are fictional as are Jamie, the escaped slave boy, and Jebediah, Melinda's husband.

John Singleton, former Corporal, Co. F., 25th North Carolina is historical. He was wounded at the Crater in 1864 and survived his wounds. His marriage to Annie Parker, his friendships in Pittsburgh, and his move to the North are not historical.

Captain Goldman Bryson, 1st Tennessee National Guard, is historical. He assisted Unionist and Confederate deserters in their escape to Kentucky. Tom and Caleb escaping to Tennessee with Bryson's help is historically consistent.

Tinker Dave Beatty, William Clift, and the Reverend Bill Carter were Unionist guerrillas in East Tennessee. Carter's brothers and their positions in the Federal army were real, as was Carter's participation in the East Tennessee and Virginia Railroad raid that destroyed the bridges. It is likely that neither Beatty nor Carter were in any way involved in the battle of Perryville.

The Parker carbine is fictional, but the Spencer on which it is based was a Civil War weapon. The Spencer fired rim-fire bullets that could not be reused. A Confederate who captured one of these guns could use it only as long as he had ammunition. Southern munitions makers had no ability to produce rim-fire bullets.

In making a center, or pin, fire-based carbine, Tom and Caleb could have fired any .44 caliber bullet. Scarcity of this ammunition was an issue. Giving the Parker boys the ability to make their own bullets acknowledged this concern.

Champ Ferguson, the Confederate bushwhacker, also was real. He and Tinker Dave feuded before the war. The story about Tinker Dave's raid on the Bledsoe farm is historical. Guerrillas, Unionists, and bushwhackers on both sides were vicious. Champ Ferguson has the dubious distinction of being the only partisan on either side to be hanged for criminal acts after the war.

The story about John Hunt Morgan's lieutenant, Rains Philpot, and Champ Ferguson also is true. They simply took the men into the woods and shot them. Such behavior occurred on both sides among guerrillas. Likewise, the Tazewell engagement is factual except to accommodate the presence of the men under Carter and Beatty. DeCourcy's execution of the Union soldiers and partisans is factual. They simply murdered their prisoners in cold blood.

There was a Union cavalry raid into Haywood County, North Carolina, in September 1862. None of the Yankee cavalrymen hanged any locals. There were a number of people who were shot and considerable destruction of property.

Both the battle of Chancellorsville and the night assault on Culp's Hill have been described as accurately as possible. The officer cupping his hands to scream orders at the men of the 75th Ohio at Chancellorsville was Colonel Robert Riley, who actually died in the battle. Bill Southerton was the Union soldier who fired on the Confederate Captain and survived the battle.

Lee's withdrawal of the Army of Northern Virginia is similarly consistent with historical fact. All of the men from the 26th North Carolina survived Gettysburg. Lee Ballou actually was wounded in action during the battle. Reed Wyatt was promoted to lieutenant in the Confederate cavalry. George Grimsley received his commission as an officer on September 9, 1864. The events of the Caleb's journey as far as Asheville are contrived.

All of the stories about O.T. Higgins and his family are true. Caleb saving Frank from wild dogs is fiction. The old town of Rushford is at the bottom of Rushford Lake. Rushford now is located northwest of the lake.

Caleb's welcome by the 23rd Virginia at the 50th Gettysburg anniversary reflects descriptions of actual events. Black Confederates were unexpected and no plans for them were made. When they arrived, their comrades shared their tents and supplies.

The existence of black Confederate soldiers is hotly contested. Lewis Steiner of the U.S. Sanitary Commission, a Yankee, counted 3,000 such troops among Jackson's Corps in 1862. He explicitly distinguished them from cooks, body servants, and logistical support slaves and free blacks. Specifically, three things were noted: their uniform buttons, arms, and the fact that they were marching in the ranks.

Body servants taking the place of dead masters cannot account for Steiner's tally. Slave soldiers were explicity prohibited until 1865. Confederate naval records and anecdotal sources also point to the large numbers of blacks as soldiers and sailors. The existence of 251,000 free persons of color in the South provides a possible explanation. Demographic data support the likelihood of ten percent (25,000) of this population enlisting in the Confederate forces.

Their reasons for fighting may have been no more complex than those attributed to Caleb. They fought to defend their homes or prove their loyalty to their communities. More fundamentally, they may have fought to gain greater equality based solely on their humanity. The war emancipated the slaves, but cost them dearly in the century that followed.

Reconstructed Yankee weaves as much historical fact into the storyline as possible to increase its credibility among readers with an active interest in the Southern War for Independence. That goal could not be attained without the research of serious academicians. I offer specific thanks to John C. Inscoe and Gordon B. McKinney, Ernest B. Furguson, and Harry W. Phanz, whose works provided significant information.

The first hymn sung at Tom Parker's funeral is "We Conquer or Die." It was composed and arranged for the pianoforte in 1861 by James Pierpoint (1822-1893). The words to the second hymn, "Mercy," were written in 1854 by George W. Doane (1799-1859).

My editors, Drs. William Adams and Betty Burnett, have earned special thanks. Without their respective efforts, Caleb's story would not have gained its current quality.

My special thanks go also to Drew Pallo, who produced the sketch of Caleb Parker. His artistry is only part of his contribution to this book. Drew, the use of your library in my research is genuinely appreciated. Of greater value is your support and encouragement for each of our book projects. Dwain Skinner prepared the maps for this book. Dwain, many thanks.

Living with a writer is difficult enough. Living with a writer who also has a full-time job is frustrating, if not impossible. As this book was being written, my wife also was contending with our then nine-month-old son, TJ. Since our household includes four other children—Ashleigh, Michael, Joseph, and Megan—considerable patience is needed. For Debbie, thank you. I love you, darling.

FURTHER READING

Several books are suggested to those interested in the mountain community and Southern Unionist apsects of the Civil War era. The number of books published since 1997 is indicative of increased scholarship in the region.

Fisher, Noel C., *War at Every Door: Partisan Politics and Guerrilla Violence in East Tennessee, 1860-1869*, University of North Carolina Press, 1997.

Freeling, William W., *The South vs. The South: How Anti-Confederate Southerners Shaped the Course of the Civil War*, Oxford University Press, 2001.

Furguson, Ernest B., *Chancellorsville 1863: The Souls of the Brave*, Alfred A. Knopf, 1992.

Groce, W. Todd, *Mountain Rebels: East Tennessee Confederates and the Civil War*, University of Tennessee Press, 1999.

Inscoe, John C. and McKinney, Gordon B., *The Heart of Confederate Appalachia: Western North Carolina in the Civil War*, University of North Carolina Press, 2000.

Jordan, Ervin L., *Black Confederates and Afro-Yankees in Civil War Virginia*, University Press of Virginia, 1995.

O'Brien, Sean Michael, *Mountain Partisans: Guerrilla Warfare in the Southern Appalachians, 1861-1865*, Praeger, 1999.

Pfantz, Harry W., *Gettysburg: Culp's Hill and Cemetery Hill*, University of North Carolina Press, 1993.

Rollins, Richards, *Black Southerners in Gray: Essays on Afro-Americans in Confederate Armies*, Southern Heritage Press, 1994.

Sutherland, Daniel E., (ed.), et. al., *Guerrillas, Unionists, and Violence on the Confederate Home Front*, University of Arkansas Press, 1999.